Getting Sympathy

"Hi, Lizzie," Jessica said as she hopped off her bike. "What's up?"

"Why did you tell Caroline Pearce that Mom is dying?" Elizabeth asked.

Jessica's mouth fell open. "Dying! I never said that!"

"Well, what did you tell her?"

"Let's see . . . I guess I told her that Mom is sick. And that we're not sure what's wrong with her."

"Jessica, how could you? You know how Caroline loves to stretch the truth. Homeroom hasn't even started yet, and she's already told half the school that Mom's dying!"

Jessica gasped. She felt shocked and embarrassed. But at the same time, she couldn't help feeling just a tiny bit pleased. Over the last few days she'd been so worried about her mother she could hardly stand it. I deserve a little sympathy, she thought. We both do.

Bantam Books in the SWEET VALLEY TWINS series
Ask your bookseller for the books you have missed

SWEET VALLEY TWINS

Centre of Attention

Written by
Jamie Suzanne

Created by
FRANCINE PASCAL

BANTAM BOOKS
TORONTO · NEW YORK · LONDON · SYDNEY · AUCKLAND

CENTRE OF ATTENTION
A BANTAM BOOK 0 553 17527 0

First publication in Great Britain

PRINTING HISTORY
Bantam edition published 1988

Bantam Books are published by Transworld Publishers
Ltd., 61–63 Uxbridge Road, Ealing, London W5 5SA, in
Australia by Transworld Publishers (Australia) Pty. Ltd.,
15–23 Helles Avenue, Moorebank, NSW 2170, and in New
Zealand by Transworld Publishers (N.Z.) Ltd., Cnr. Moselle
and Waipareira Avenues, Henderson, Auckland.

Printed and bound in Great Britain by
Cox & Wyman Ltd., Reading, Berks.

With thanks to
Herman Weiss, Ph.D.,
and A. Lawrence Ossias, M.D.

One

◇

Jessica Wakefield rode her bicycle down her shady, tree-lined street. She turned into the driveway of her split-level ranch house and let herself in through the kitchen door.

The first person she saw was her fourteen-year-old brother, Steven. He was standing by the refrigerator with a basketball tucked under one arm, gulping down a soda.

"Steven, guess what I saw at the mall today?" Jessica said eagerly.

"A UFO?" Steven suggested with a smirk.

"No, silly," she said. "I saw just the sweater I've been looking for. The most perfect sweater—"

"'The most *perfect* sweater,'" he mimicked in a high voice. "Oh, Mom, I'll just die if I can't have it!"

He tossed his empty soda can into the trash and burst out laughing.

"Steven!" Jessica swiped at him, but he jumped out of reach. He was still laughing as he ran out the back door.

Jessica frowned. She should have known better than to expect Steven to care about her news. All he lived for was basketball and food.

Jessica put down her books and walked into the living room. From there, she could hear her mother and her twin sister, Elizabeth, talking in the den.

"You know, Mom, I love working on *The Sweet Valley Sixers*," Elizabeth was saying, "but someday I want to write other things, too. I'd like to write a horse story, like *Black Beauty*."

"Well, why don't you give it a try?" Mrs. Wakefield said. "You have a terrific imagination. I know you'd do a good job."

Jessica rolled her eyes. *Sometimes Elizabeth can be so dull!* she thought. *All she ever talks about is reading, writing, and that dumb old sixth-grade newspaper.*

Jessica and Elizabeth were identical twins. They both had long, sun-streaked blond hair, blue-green eyes, and a tiny dimple in their left cheeks. But that is where the similarities ended. Since entering Sweet Valley Middle School, they no longer dressed alike. Elizabeth wore her hair pulled back from her face. Her clothes were casual, and she never bothered with makeup. But Jessica had started to wear her hair down in loose waves. Her clothes were always coordinated and fashionable, and she wore lip gloss and a touch of mascara as well.

The girls were different in other ways, too. Elizabeth was thoughtful. She loved to read and have long talks with her friends. Jessica, however, was impatient and moved more quickly. She loved clothes and gossip, and she spent all her free time with the Unicorns, an exclusive club made up of all of her good friends. Elizabeth thought Jessica's friends were stuck up, and Jessica thought Elizabeth's friends were too serious. But deep down, the twins respected their differences, and they were the best of friends.

Elizabeth and her mother were still talking when Jessica came barrelling into the den. "Guess what?" she announced, barely containing her excitement. "I saw the most beautiful sweater at the mall today!"

Elizabeth was sitting on the couch. "I'll bet it's purple," she said with a smile. Purple was the Unicorn Club's favorite color, and all the members tried to wear something purple every day. Elizabeth thought it was a silly idea.

"It's pale, pale violet," Jessica said, "with a white unicorn embroidered across the front." She turned to her mother. "Oh, Mom, if I had that sweater, all of the Unicorns would be *so* jealous. I've got to have it!"

"It sounds lovely," Mrs. Wakefield said, easing

back in a recliner chair, "but can we talk about it later? I had a rough day at work, and I feel terribly tired."

"But, Mom—" Jessica began.

"I called your father, and he's bringing home Chinese food for dinner," Mrs. Wakefield continued. "I think I'll just take a short nap before he gets here." She rested her head against the back of the chair and yawned.

"Come on," Elizabeth whispered. She stood up and took Jessica's arm. "Let's let Mom get some rest."

Jessica frowned and followed Elizabeth out of the room. She felt angry and hurt. Her mother had just spent plenty of time talking with Elizabeth. But as soon as Jessica wanted to talk, her mother had no time.

"You know, I'm worried about Mom," Elizabeth said after they had left the room. "She seems awfully tired lately."

"So?" Jessica said irritably.

"It's just funny, that's all," Elizabeth said with a shrug. "Mom never takes a nap before dinner."

"Well, it doesn't surprise me," Jessica said. "Your nonstop talking probably wore her out."

Elizabeth looked hurt, but Jessica didn't care. She didn't like being ignored, especially by her own mother.

Jessica went into the kitchen and poured herself some juice. Then she had an idea. Maybe she could make a special dessert for dinner. That way her mother would surely pay attention to her. Eagerly, she opened the closet and took out the Unicorns' celebrity cookbook. A few months ago, the club had written letters to celebrities in order to find out their favorite recipes. Then they'd collected the recipes into a book and sold it to raise money for a dance.

Jessica flipped through the book until she came to a recipe for chocolate parfait, sent in by movie star Leslie Morgan. It looked easy and quick. She got out the ingredients and set to work.

At dinner, Mr. Wakefield told the family he had an announcement to make. "I'm going to New York City on business in a few days," he said. "I'll be gone for about two weeks."

"What case are you working on?" Steven asked between bites of egg roll. Mr. Wakefield was a successful lawyer with an office in Sweet Valley.

"It's for the My-T-Good Chocolate Company in Los Angeles. They think a company in New York has stolen their coconut candy bar recipe. I'm going to meet with the New York company and see if we can work things out."

"And will you get to sample a lot of candy bars while you're there?" Elizabeth asked.

"I'll save that job for your mother," Mr. Wakefield said. "She's coming with me for the first week of the trip. We've asked your Great-aunt Shirley to come to Sweet Valley and look after you."

"I hope I can shake this cold before we leave," Mrs. Wakefield said. She rubbed her eyes. "I won't make a very good traveling companion if I feel this worn-out."

Mr. Wakefield looked concerned. "That cold has been dragging on for some time. Don't you think you'd better see the doctor?"

"I will if I don't feel better soon."

Jessica tapped her fingers against the table. She was impatient for the meal to end so she could surprise her mother with dessert. Then, when everyone had finished telling her how delicious it tasted, Jessica would ask her parents for the money to buy the unicorn sweater.

Finally, Mr. Wakefield pushed back his chair. "I'll be in my study," he said. "I have a lot of paperwork to do for my trip."

"Wait!" Jessica cried. "I made a special dessert. It's chocolate parfait."

"Yum!" exclaimed Elizabeth.

Steven groaned. "If Jessica made it, it probably tastes like mud."

"Steven," Mr. Wakefield scolded. He turned to Jessica. "That sounds delicious, Jessica. I'll take mine with me into the study."

Jessica looked expectantly at her mother. But Mrs. Wakefield just smiled and said, "That was a nice surprise, honey, but I'm too full to eat another bite." She yawned and added, "I'm going upstairs to lie down."

"But, Mom," Jessica began, "I wanted to ask you about that sweater. . . ."

Mrs. Wakefield stood up and patted Jessica's shoulder. "Ask me later, OK?"

Before Jessica could answer, her mother turned and walked out of the room.

Jessica spent the evening in her bedroom, doing her homework. She was having trouble concentrating, though. *Why is Mom ignoring me?* she wondered, feeling frustrated and unhappy. It just wasn't fair.

Just then, there was a knock at her bedroom door. "Can I come in?" Elizabeth asked through the door.

"No. Go away," Jessica said grumpily. There was no reason to be angry with Elizabeth, but she couldn't help it. It bothered her that her mother had taken the time to talk to Elizabeth, but not to her.

"It's important," Elizabeth said. "I want to talk to you."

"Oh, all right," Jessica muttered. "Come in. But make it quick. I'm busy."

Elizabeth opened the door and walked into Jessica's room. Until recently, the girls had shared a bedroom. That was when Elizabeth thought twins should do everything together. Now she was glad she had her own room, because she liked things neat and orderly. Her books were carefully arranged on her bookshelves, and her clothes were hung neatly in her closet. Jessica's room, on the other hand, looked as if a cyclone had just passed through. Clothes were strewn across the floor, papers were spilling off the desk, and there were magazines and bubble-gum wrappers on the bed.

"It's about Mom," Elizabeth said, closing the door behind her. She pushed aside a pile of fashion magazines and sat down on her sister's bed. "Does she seem any different to you?"

"How should I know? *You're* the one she talks to, not me."

Elizabeth frowned. "What do you mean?"

"She hasn't paid any attention to me all day," Jessica complained. "I tried to tell her about the sweater I saw at the mall, but she was barely listening. She'd rather listen to you."

"That's not true," Elizabeth answered. "Mom hasn't had much time for me, either. Just yesterday I asked her if she'd help me hem my new jeans, but she told me she was too tired. Then tonight after dinner I took some tea to her, and she dozed off while I was in there!"

Jessica wasn't about to dismiss the whole thing so easily. But the more she thought about it, the more it seemed that Elizabeth was right. Their mother *did* seem unusually tired lately. And she seemed to have less time for both of them. "Remember last weekend when Dad drove us up to Secca Lake," she said at last. "Mom didn't feel like coming with us."

"That's exactly what I'm talking about," Elizabeth said. "Mom just hasn't been herself lately."

"Well, she has a cold. At least that's what she said at dinner," Jessica said hopefully.

"I know," Elizabeth answered, "but she isn't

sneezing or coughing. She only seems tired all the time."

Just then, Mr. Wakefield knocked at the door. "Girls," he called. "Time for bed."

Normally, Jessica liked having her own room just as much as Elizabeth did. But right now she wished her twin didn't have to leave. She wanted to keep talking.

Elizabeth stood up. "OK, Daddy. I'm on my way!" She turned to her sister and gave her a sympathetic look. "We'll talk some more tomorrow." Then she walked through the bathroom that separated the twins' bedrooms and closed the door.

After Elizabeth left, Jessica changed into her nightgown and thought about what her sister had said. *Maybe Mom isn't ignoring me after all*, she decided.

She got into bed and pulled the covers up to her chin. Her mother had been complaining about her cold for weeks. But if it was just a simple cold, why was it dragging on for so long?

Jessica couldn't shake the uneasy feeling in the pit of her stomach. Closing her eyes, she lay there a long time before she finally drifted off to sleep.

Two

◇

"Jessica! Elizabeth! Wake up, girls," Mrs. Wakefield called, knocking on the twins' bedroom doors. "I'm leaving for work early today so I can catch up on a few things."

Jessica opened her eyes and glanced at her alarm clock. It was seven-thirty. Normally, her mother's part-time job at Sweet Valley Design didn't start until nine o'clock. *Good*, Jessica thought. *If Mom's leaving for work this early, she must be feeling better.*

"Mom wouldn't be going to work if she didn't feel well," Jessica announced happily to her sister on their way to school. "Especially not so early."

"I guess you're right," Elizabeth agreed as they

crossed the street to the Sweet Valley Middle School lawn. "It just seems—"

But before she could continue, a boy on a bike came whizzing out of nowhere. "Out of my way!" he yelled, pedaling toward them. Jessica and Elizabeth leaped to the sidewalk just in time.

"Watch where you're going!" Jessica shouted as the boy tore off down the street.

"Who was that?" Elizabeth asked, struggling to catch her breath.

"Dennis Cookman, I think," Jessica answered. Dennis was a seventh grader, but he looked big enough to be in high school. He was tall, with broad shoulders.

"He only missed us by a couple of inches," Elizabeth said.

Jessica made a face. "What a jerk!"

When the twins reached the wide, grassy lawn, they split up, as they did almost every morning. Elizabeth went off to talk to her friends on the staff of *The Sweet Valley Sixers*, while Jessica hurried to find her fellow Unicorns.

Ever since she'd been asked to join the Unicorns at the beginning of sixth grade, Jessica had felt special. They were the prettiest and most popular girls in school. And since most of them were seventh and eighth graders, being with them made Jessica feel very important.

Today, Lila Fowler and Ellen Riteman were standing beside the flagpole, talking and laughing. Jessica hurried to join them.

"Did you hear the news?" Ellen asked eagerly as Jessica walked up. "The school is doing a production of *Carnival*! Auditions are in two weeks."

"Isn't that a musical? What's it about?" Jessica asked.

"I watched the video last month on my new projection TV," Lila Fowler said importantly. Lila was from one of the wealthier families in Sweet Valley, and she loved to brag about the expensive things her father bought her. "It's about an orphan girl named Lily. She joins a traveling carnival and falls in love with a handsome magician."

"Ooh, it sounds romantic!" Jessica exclaimed.

"It is," Lila said with a nod. "The magician breaks her heart, and she ends up with a puppeteer who always loved her."

Jessica started to imagine herself as the star of *Carnival*. She pictured herself up on the stage, sobbing because the cruel magician had broken her heart. It sounded so dramatic! The musical was going to be the most thrilling thing that had happened at Sweet Valley Middle School in ages. By the time she reached her homeroom, Jessica knew she had to be a part of it.

At lunch, Jessica joined her friends at their regular table.

"Did you hear?" Kimberly Haver asked, pushing back her thick black hair. "Dennis Cookman stole Jimmy Underwood's bicycle!"

Jessica's eyes widened. "I saw Dennis Cookman riding a bike this morning. He practically ran Lizzie and me over. Do you think it was Jimmy's bike?"

"It must have been," Kimberly said. "Jimmy parked his bike outside the Elm Street Quick-Mart while he went in to buy a comic book. When he walked out, Dennis was riding away on it."

"Dennis is going to get in big trouble," Ellen Riteman said.

Lila shrugged. "I'm not so sure. Jimmy is really shy. He probably won't even tell on Dennis. Besides, Dennis is about twice his size."

The girls ate in silence for a minute. Then Jessica said, "Just two weeks until the *Carnival* auditions. Doesn't it sound exciting?"

"Someone from the Unicorns should audition for the lead," Janet Howell said. Janet was president of the Unicorns, and she liked to make sure the club members were always the center of attention.

"That's right," Kimberly said, taking a sip of milk. "The girl who plays Lily should be very pretty and very special. Just like the Unicorns."

"Well, who in the Unicorns is a good actress?" Janet asked.

"Jessica is," Ellen piped up. She looked at Jessica. "You danced the lead in your ballet recital, right?"

"But that was dancing, not acting." Janet protested.

"I had to act, too," Jessica said proudly. "The other girls played life-size dolls, but I was the heroine, Swanilda."

"That sounds like a scene from *Carnival*!" Lila

said excitedly. "Lily dreams that the puppeteer's puppets have come to life. She does a dance with them."

"Oh, Jess, you'd be perfect!" Kimberly exclaimed.

Jessica could hardly contain her excitement. The role *did* sound perfect for her. She pictured herself on stage, dancing with the life-size puppets and the audience jumping to their feet to give her a standing ovation.

"I heard Dana Larson talking about the auditions in gym class today," Ellen said. "She said she's going to try out for the part of Lily."

Dana was a tall, thin girl with short blond hair and a pointy chin. She had a strong, clear soprano voice.

"But she's not as pretty as Jessica," Ellen remarked.

Jessica smiled. She loved the Unicorns. Being in such an exclusive club made her feel wanted and special. It almost made her feel better than girls like Dana Larson. *And if I win the role of Lily,* she thought, *that will prove it.*

"Did you see the latest copy of *The Sweet Valley Sixers*?" Ellen said, pulling the newspaper out of her backpack. "Listen to what it says in Caroline Pearce's gossip column." She opened the paper and read, "*'Dana Larson will be trying out for the part of Lily, and Bruce Patman is a shoo-in for the role of the magician.'*"

Jessica's eyes widened. Bruce Patman was the cutest boy in the whole seventh grade!

"Bruce is so dreamy!" Janet cried.

"Imagine if you got the part, Jessica," Kimberly said. "You might even get to kiss him!" The girls all burst into excited giggles.

"Can't you just picture it?" Ellen said, turning to Jessica. "You and Bruce step to the edge of the stage for the curtain call. The audience is cheering, and Bruce hands you a bouquet of beautiful red roses!"

Right then and there, Jessica decided she was going to get that part—no matter what!

After school, Jessica went to Madame Andre's studio for her ballet lesson.

"Jessica," Madame Andre said before the class began, "your mother has called. She's not feeling well today, so she arranged for you to ride home with Kerry Glenn."

Jessica frowned. This morning she had been positive her mother was feeling much better. But now she wasn't so sure. She thought about what Elizabeth had said the night before. *"Mom just hasn't been herself lately."* It was true. It just wasn't like her mother to be sick for so long.

Kerry was at the barre, doing her stretching exercises. Jessica joined her. She stretched her leg across the barre and leaned over until her head was resting on her knee.

"Hi," Kerry said. She tossed her long, dark braid over her shoulder and smiled. "Madame Andre told me you're getting a ride with me today."

Jessica nodded. "My mother's sick."

"That's too bad. What's wrong?"

"I'm not sure," Jessica said between stretches. "Mostly she's just tired all the time."

"Uh-oh. Sounds exactly like my mom. She was dragging around for weeks before she found out what was wrong with her."

"What was it?" Jessica asked with interest.

"She was pregnant!"

Jessica laughed. "No way. My mom couldn't be pregnant."

"That's what I thought, too," Kerry replied. "But now I have a baby brother!"

Jessica swallowed hard. Suddenly, she wasn't so sure what to believe. After all, if it had happened to Kerry's mother, maybe it could happen to her mother, too. "How did your mom act?" she asked anxiously. "I mean, did she take a lot of naps?"

"Yes. And she always seemed to be kind of grumpy. Oh, and she felt sick to her stomach."

Jessica could hardly believe her ears. Her mother was acting exactly like that! Not only had she been tired lately, but she had been grumpy, too. Could she have passed up Jessica's special dessert because she felt sick to her stomach?

Jessica spent her entire ballet class thinking about this new possibility. When class ended, she changed out of her leotard and walked outside with Kerry. "What's it like having a baby brother?" she asked.

"Horrible!" Kerry moaned. "All he does is eat,

sleep, cry, and dirty his diapers. And yesterday he spit up all over my homework."

The girls looked up as Mrs. Glenn's car appeared around the corner. A small baby was sitting in a carseat in the back, screaming and crying. "Hurry up, girls!" Mrs. Glenn called, pulling up to the curb. "It's time for the baby's feeding. Kerry, see if you can keep him quiet until we get home."

Jessica's stomach started to churn. She climbed into the backseat and glanced over at Kerry's baby brother. His face was bright red and he was shrieking so loudly it made her ears hurt.

Mom can't be pregnant, Jessica thought anxiously. *She just isn't.* Then she crossed her fingers and added, *I hope.*

Three

◇

When Jessica got home, she found Elizabeth and Steven in the kitchen. "Hi, Jess," Elizabeth said, carrying a pot of water from the sink to the stove. "Mom asked us to start dinner. She's upstairs, lying down."

"Lizzie," Jessica said, rushing to her sister's side, "something awful is happening."

Steven looked up from the tomato he was cutting. "What's wrong?" he asked. "Did you get a run in your tights or something?"

"This isn't funny," Jessica insisted. "I think . . . well, maybe . . . Mom's going to have a baby!" she blurted out.

"A baby!" Elizabeth gasped. She turned from

the stove and stared at her sister. "You've got to be kidding!"

"I'm not," Jessica answered urgently. "Listen, she's tired all the time, right? Well, so was Kerry Glenn's mother. And then it turned out Mrs. Glenn was pregnant!"

"Who's pregnant?" Mrs. Wakefield asked, walking into the kitchen.

"Our brilliant sister says *you* are," Steven answered.

Mrs. Wakefield laughed. "What in the world gave you that idea?"

"You've been so tired lately," Jessica began. "I was just worried—"

"Well, don't be," Mrs. Wakefield said, giving Jessica an affectionate hug. "I'm just a little run down, that's all. Just give me a few more days, and I'll be back to normal."

Steven went back to cutting tomatoes. "A baby!" he said, smirking. "Boy, Jessica, you sure come up with some dumb ideas."

"I'm just glad I was wrong," Jessica replied. She made a face at Steven and added, "One brother is enough."

"Yeah, well, one sister is enough, too," he shot back. "So why don't you do us all a favor and . . .?"

"All right, you two," Mrs. Wakefield interrupted. Then she smiled and said, "I can take over from here. Thanks for your help."

"Are you sure?" Elizabeth asked.

"Absolutely. I'm feeling much better. Now, go on. I'll call you when dinner's ready."

Elizabeth and Steven left the kitchen, but Jessica stayed. She was so relieved her mother wasn't pregnant that she felt like cheering. She grabbed a spoon and sampled the spaghetti sauce her mother was stirring. "Hmm," she said, "delicious!"

Mrs. Wakefield tasted a spoonful. "Not bad. Not bad at all." She smiled and added, "Set the table, please. We'll be eating in ten minutes."

It was Elizabeth's turn to set the table, but Jessica was feeling too happy to complain. "Guess what, Mom?" she announced. "We're putting on a production of *Carnival* at school, and I'm going to audition for the lead!"

"That sounds like fun," Mrs. Wakefield said. She handed Jessica a stack of plates. "*Carnival* has always been one of my favorite musicals. I remember seeing the movie when I was about your age. I knew all the songs by heart."

Jessica walked into the dining room and began setting the table. Maybe they could rent the movie from the video store at the mall, she thought. Then suddenly she remembered that there was something else she wanted from the mall—something much more exciting than a videotape. "Remember that sweater I told you about?" she called to her mother. "The one I saw in the mall?"

"Yes, I seem to remember you saying something about a sweater," Mrs. Wakefield replied.

"It's beautiful, Mom," Jessica said eagerly. "It's violet with a white unicorn embroidered across the front." She walked back into the kitchen. "Mom, it's just perfect for me."

Mrs. Wakefield looked up from her spaghetti sauce. "How much does it cost?" she asked.

"Well . . . um . . . not much really. Just, uh, forty dollars."

Mrs. Wakefield frowned. "That's quite a bit of money. Especially for something you don't really need."

"But, Mom," Jessica cried, "I *do* need it. Don't you see? Any Unicorn would die to have a sweater like that one. And there was only one in the whole store. Can't I have it, Mom? Please?"

"I'll tell you what," Mrs. Wakefield said. "If you save your allowance until you have twenty dollars, your father and I will give you the rest."

Jessica groaned. She hated saving money. In fact, she usually spent her allowance the same day she got it. "But, Mom," she pleaded, "it will take me weeks and weeks to save that much money. And by that time the sweater will be gone. Couldn't you just buy it for me and let me pay you back later?"

"That wouldn't teach you the value of saving," Mrs. Wakefield said calmly. "Now, come on, honey, finish setting the table."

Jessica sighed loudly. It just wasn't fair. It was going to take forever to save the money to buy the sweater—*if* one of the other girls in the Unicorns didn't buy it first. "It's Elizabeth's turn to set the table," Jessica called grumpily. "Ask her to finish." Then she turned and stomped out of the room.

When the twins walked into their homeroom the next morning, their teacher, Mr. Davis was standing by the door. "Line up, everyone," he said. "There's no homeroom this morning. We're having a special assembly instead. Something about the school musical."

"Are you going to try out?" Jessica asked Elizabeth as the class walked down the hall to the auditorium.

"No, I don't think so," Elizabeth replied. "But I'm going to write a series about the show for the *Sixers*. Sort of a behind-the-scenes look at the whole production. One article will be about the scenery, then the costumes, the music, the stars—"

"Then you can interview me," Jessica said. "I'm trying out for the lead!"

"That's great, Jess!" Elizabeth exclaimed, giving her twin's arm a squeeze. "Good luck."

When everyone was seated in the auditorium, Mr. Clark, the principal, walked out onto the stage. "*Carnival* will be the middle school's first musical production," he said proudly, "and we're all very excited. But to make it a success, we need everyone's help. And now, I'll let Ms. McDonald tell you how you can get involved."

Ms. McDonald, the school's music teacher, stepped up to the microphone.

Jessica sat up straight in her chair and listened closely.

"Auditions will be after school a week from Friday," Ms. McDonald began. "You will be judged on your acting and singing ability. Everyone who's trying out should come prepared to sing one song. It doesn't need to be a song from *Carnival*—just a song that shows off your voice. Remember, a musical succeeds or fails on the strength of its singing. We need voices that will make the audience sit up and take notice! We also need help with scenery, costumes, publicity, and much, much more."

Ms. McDonald was still talking, but Jessica was too busy thinking about the audition to listen. It wasn't the acting that concerned her. She was pretty sure she could handle that. It was the singing.

Jessica twirled a strand of hair around her fingers thoughtfully. Her voice wasn't bad, she knew that. She could carry a tune, and she almost never sang off-key. But was it the kind of voice that would make an audience sit up and take notice? And, even more important, was it as good as Dana Larson's?

When the assembly ended, Jessica walked out of the auditorium and looked for the other Unicorns. Instead, she saw Caroline Pearce. Caroline was the biggest gossip at Sweet Valley Middle School. Her weekly column in *The Sweet Valley Sixers* was full of juicy rumors about students and teachers, and she was always in search of new tidbits. "Hi, Jessica," she called, pushing through the crowd. "Did you hear about Jimmy Underwood?"

"What about him?"

"When he walked out of his house this morning, he found his bike lying on the front lawn. The handlebars were bent, and it had two flat tires."

"I bet Dennis Cookman ran it into a tree or something," Jessica said. "The way he was riding yesterday I wouldn't be surprised."

"Yes, I heard he almost ran you over." Caroline patted her long red hair and fixed her sharp green eyes on Jessica. "And that's not all I heard. Janet Howell told me you're trying out for the lead in *Carnival.*"

Jessica nodded. "That's right."

"Ooh, how exciting! That makes you and Dana Larson the two top contenders." She paused thoughtfully. "Of course, Dana does have a fabulous voice." She moved closer to Jessica and whispered, "But I overheard Bruce Patman telling Charlie Cashman he wanted *you* to get the part."

"You did?" Jessica asked breathlessly.

Caroline smiled and nodded. "Oh, there's Elise," she said suddenly, catching sight of her friend. "See you later, Jess," she called, hurrying into the crowd.

Jessica walked down the hall, barely noticing the people around her. According to Caroline's gossip column, Bruce Patman was a shoo-in for the role of the magician. And he wanted Jessica to be Lily!

At dinner that evening, Mr. Wakefield told the family that he was leaving for New York the following morning. "I'll be on my way to the airport before any of you kids are awake," he said. "So we'll have to say goodbye to each other tonight."

"But when is Aunt Sally coming?" Elizabeth asked.

"She's not," Mrs. Wakefield answered. "Your father and I talked it over, and we decided I'm going to stay here."

"Are you kidding?" Steven exclaimed. "And give up a chance to eat all those candy bars?"

Mrs. Wakefield smiled. "I'd rather go, believe me. But this silly cold has made me fall behind at work, and I just can't afford to take time off. Besides, I'm really not up to a big trip right now."

"But are you sure you're up to taking care of three children all by yourself?" Mr. Wakefield asked.

"Don't be silly, Ned. I'm not that sick."

"Well, all right," Mr. Wakefield said, looking worried. "But call me in New York if you have any problems. I can always come home early if I have to."

Jessica exchanged a look with her sister. Her parents' conversation was making her uneasy, and from the way Elizabeth was frowning, Jessica knew she felt the same way.

Mr. Wakefield turned to the twins and Steven. "Be good while I'm gone. Help your mother out, and don't give her any trouble, OK?"

But before they could answer, Mrs. Wakefield smiled mischievously and said, "Oh, don't worry about us. We're going to have a great time while you're gone, aren't we, kids? We'll eat chocolate cake for dinner. And we'll stay up all night and watch videos."

"Right," Steven laughed, joining in. "And we'll throw a big party and invite the entire high school!"

"And we won't wash any dishes!" Mrs. Wakefield cried. "We'll just leave them for your father when he gets home!"

By now the whole family was laughing. Jessica joined in eagerly. Looking around the table at her parents' happy faces, it seemed silly to be worried. But deep inside, she still wished her father didn't have to go away.

Four

◇

Two days later, Jessica was riding her bike home from school. As she pedaled, she practiced the song she had chosen to sing at her *Carnival* audition. It was an upbeat number called "Look at Me" from *Shout*, a musical she'd seen in Los Angeles. "Hey, world," she sang as she rode along, "look at me, me, me! I'm gonna shout what I'm about, for everyone to see!"

Jessica sighed. Her voice was clear and true, but it sounded much too thin and delicate. She'd never win the lead if she sang like that.

She threw her head back and tried again. "Hey, world!" she bellowed as she pedaled up the driveway to her house. "Look at me, me, me!"

When Jessica walked in the kitchen door, she was still singing. Just then the phone started to ring.

Quickly, she tossed her books on the counter and answered it.

"Hello," a woman's voice said, "this is Dr. Costa's office. Is Mrs. Wakefield there?"

Dr. Costa was the Wakefields' family doctor. *Why would Dr. Costa's office be calling?* she wondered. "Uh, Mrs. Wakefield isn't here right now," she said. "Can I take a message?"

"Just tell her we have the results of her blood test," the woman replied.

Jessica's heart thudded against her ribs. She hadn't heard anything about her mother going to the doctor for a blood test. Suddenly, an awful thought came to her. What if her mother didn't have a cold? What if she was really sick—sicker than anyone realized?

"Jessica," Mrs. Wakefield called from upstairs. "Who's on the phone?"

Jessica gasped with surprise. She hadn't expected her mother to be home yet. Thinking quickly, she said to the woman on the phone, "Hold on. My mother just walked in the door." Then she held the receiver away from her ear and called upstairs, "It's for you, Mom."

Jessica knew she should hang up as soon as she heard her mother's voice. Still, if her mother was really sick, Jessica felt she had a right to know.

"Hello," she heard her mother say into the phone. "This is Alice Wakefield."

Jessica pressed her hand over the mouthpiece and listened.

"Mrs. Wakefield, this is Dr. Costa's office. We have the results of your blood test. Everything looks fine except your white blood cell count. It's slightly elevated."

"What does that mean?" Mrs. Wakefield asked.

"Probably nothing, but Dr. Costa would like you to make an appointment to have that lump on your neck biopsied—just in case. Can you come in tomorrow?"

Quietly, Jessica hung up the phone. She had no idea what all this meant, but it sounded kind of scary. She was still standing by the phone when Elizabeth and Steven came in through the back door.

"What's the matter with you?" Steven asked. "You look like your best friend just died."

"This is no time to make jokes," Jessica snapped.

Elizabeth frowned. "What's wrong, Jess? You look upset."

"Dr. Costa's office just called to talk to Mom," Jessica said in a near-whisper. "I heard the woman say—"

"You mean you listened in on the conversation?" Elizabeth exclaimed. "Jessica, that's not very nice!"

"What's not very nice?" Mrs. Wakefield asked, coming into the kitchen.

Jessica wasn't sure what to say. If she admitted she had overheard the phone conversation, her mother would be angry with her. But if she didn't, how could she find out if her mother was really sick? Finally, she said, "I didn't know you were home, so when I answered the phone just now, I asked the lady if I could take a message. She said she had the results of your blood test."

"A blood test?" Elizabeth asked. "What for?"

"Yeah," Steven said, "what's going on, Mom?"

"Probably nothing," Mrs. Wakefield replied. "Let's go into the dining room and I'll explain."

Jessica, Elizabeth, and Steven sat down solemnly at the dining room table.

"At work yesterday I was still feeling very tired," Mrs. Wakefield began. "At first I just assumed it was because of my cold—but as the morning went on, I felt worse. I was achy and hot, and finally I had to come home. That afternoon I went to see Dr. Costa. He said I had a lump on the back of my neck that was a swollen lymph node, and he gave me a blood test. The nurse just called to tell me the test isn't completely normal."

"What does that mean?" Jessica asked anxiously.

"We don't know yet," Mrs. Wakefield said gently. "It probably means I have some kind of virus. When the virus is gone, the lump will disappear."

"When will you know for sure, Mom?" Elizabeth asked.

"Soon. Tomorrow Dr. Costa is going to do some more tests. When he gets the results, he'll know what to do."

"Are you going to call Dad tonight?" Steven asked. "Maybe he'll want to come home early."

Mrs. Wakefield shook her head. "I'll talk to him

later this week. There's no need for him to come home for something as minor as this."

"But, Mom," Jessica asked, "are you sure you're going to be all right?"

"Of course I am, honey," Mrs. Wakefield reached out and squeezed Jessica's hand. "I'm going to be just fine. I promise."

Jessica smiled. The touch of her mother's hand was reassuring.

Mrs. Wakefield stood up from the dining room table. "I think I'll go upstairs now and rest a bit. Can you three get dinner ready? There's a chicken casserole in the refrigerator. It just needs to be heated up. That and a salad ought to be enough."

"Sure, Mom," Steven said. "No problem."

"Do you think Mom will be OK?" Elizabeth asked after their mother had left.

"Sure," Steven said confidently. "Like she said, it's probably nothing," He was smiling, but there was a worried look in his eyes.

"I guess we'll just have to wait until tomorrow," Elizabeth said.

Jessica looked across at Elizabeth and Steven, and then stood up abruptly. "Just listen to you two," she said. "Sitting around worrying isn't going to help anything. It's up to us to take care of things until Mom feels better. Now, what can we do to help out?"

"Make dinner," Steven said. "I mean, that's what Mom told us to do, right?"

"That's a good start," Jessica replied. "Steven, I

want you to take the casserole out of the refrigerator and put it in the oven. Then you can make a salad."

"Hey, why me?" Steven demanded. "I don't know anything about cooking."

"Steven," Jessica scolded, "this is no time to act like a baby! Mom is sick and she needs our help."

"Jessica is right," Elizabeth said. "Just doing our regular chores isn't enough right now. We all have to pitch in and do whatever is needed."

"Right," Jessica agreed. "That's why I want *you* to go down to the laundry room and put in a load of wash. My red cotton blouse needs ironing, too. Mom said she'd do it, but I can't ask her now. Will you take care of it, Lizzie?"

"Well . . . all right," Elizabeth answered slowly. "But what are you going to be doing?"

"I'm going upstairs to see if Mom needs anything." She walked purposefully out of the room and headed upstairs.

Mrs. Wakefield was sitting in bed, reading a magazine. "Hi, Mom," Jessica said, walking into the room. "I just came up to see how you're doing."

"Oh, thanks, honey," her mother said. "I feel a little achy, but other than that, I'm fine."

"Let me fluff up your pillows," Jessica said. Mrs. Wakefield leaned forward while Jessica straightened the sheets and rearranged the pillows. While she worked, she said, "I don't want you to worry about the house while you're feeling sick, Mom. I'll take care of everything. You just rest and get better, OK?"

"That's very thoughtful of you, Jessica," Mrs. Wakefield said.

Jessica beamed with pleasure. Of course, she wasn't really planning to do *all* the work around the house by herself. Elizabeth and Steven would help, too. But she would organize everything, and as far as Jessica was concerned, that was the most important job of all.

"Mom," she said, sitting on the edge of the bed, "I've been working on a song for my *Carnival* audition. Can I sing it for you?"

"Why, of course, honey," Mrs. Wakefield replied. "I'd love to hear it."

Jessica cleared her throat, threw her head back, and sang, "Hey, world, look at me, me, me!"

Downstairs in the laundry room, Elizabeth tossed a load of clothes into the washing machine and turned it on. Then, with a sigh, she turned on the iron and set to work on Jessica's shirt. When she was finished, she walked up to the kitchen to help Steven with the salad.

"Where's Jessica?" she asked.

"Upstairs," Steven said with disgust. "She's been singing the same stupid song over and over for the last fifteen minutes."

Just then, Jessica's voice could be heard from the second floor, singing, "Hey, world, look at me, me, me!"

"How come she's singing while we're down here working?" Steven asked angrily.

"I thought she was going upstairs to see if Mom needed anything."

"Yeah, well it sounds like *she's* the one who needs something," Steven muttered.

Elizabeth giggled. "She's trying out for the lead in the middle school musical. Maybe she's practicing for the audition."

"Well, it's not fair," Steven said. "She's bossing us around, telling us to do this and that, and what's *she* doing to help out around here. Nothing!" He tossed down the vegetable peeler he was using to peel carrots. "I'm going upstairs to tell Mom."

"Wait," Elizabeth said, grabbing his arm. "We shouldn't bother her with our problems right now."

"You mean you're gonna let Jessica boss you around?"

Elizabeth frowned. "I don't like it any better than you do. But Mom needs rest, and she's not going to get any if we're fighting all the time."

"I guess you're right," Steven said reluctantly. "But it's just not fair."

Just then Jessica walked into the kitchen, humming the chorus of "Look at Me." When she saw Elizabeth and Steven, she stopped. "Hey, you two, knock off the small talk. We're supposed to be getting dinner ready."

"That's what I've been doing," Steven said. "Unlike some people I know."

"I've been taking care of Mom," Jessica said haughtily. "And now I'm going to sit down and make a list of all the chores that need to be done around here. Then we can divide them up among us."

"How come you get to sit around writing lists while I have to peel these stupid carrots?" Steven demanded.

"That's all right," Elizabeth interrupted, giving Steven a sharp poke in the ribs. "I'll peel them. Jessica, you go ahead and make your list. We'll take care of the salad."

Jessica smiled with satisfaction. She knew she was being bossy, but she figured she had a good reason. Her mother was sick, and there was a lot of work to be done. *Someone has to run things around here until Mom gets better*, she told herself. *So why shouldn't it be me?*

Five

◇

The next day was Saturday. Jessica got up early and set to work. First, she served her mother breakfast in bed. Then she woke up Elizabeth and Steven and gave them their work assignments for the day.

"Elizabeth, I want you to vacuum the downstairs this morning," she said, glancing at the list of chores she had written the previous evening.

"But I planned to go horseback riding this morning," Elizabeth protested. She often rode her friend Ted Rogers's horse, Thunder, at Carson Stables.

"Well, you'll just have to change your plans," Jessica replied. "We have too much work to do right here at home."

"Count me out," Steven said. "Joe Howell and I are meeting at school this morning to shoot baskets."

"Forget it," Jessica said curtly. She looked at her list. "Today I want you to wash the van and mow the lawn."

"Oh, yeah?" Steven said. "And what are you going to do, Little Miss Dictator?"

"I'm going to Dr. Costa's office with Mom," she said. "She should have someone from the family with her. And when we get back, I'll make lunch for her."

"But I thought you told me the Unicorns were going shopping at the mall today," Elizabeth reminded her sister.

Jessica had forgotten all about her shopping date with the Unicorns. "I'm not going," she said simply. "Now let's get to work."

Jessica walked downstairs and dialed Lila's number. "I can't go to the mall today," she said when her friend picked up the phone. "My mother is sick, and I have to stay home and take care of her."

"Sick?" Lila asked. "What's wrong with her?"

"We're not sure yet," Jessica said. "She's going to the doctor for a test today."

Suddenly, Jessica remembered the violet unicorn sweater. There was only one in the whole store. Jessica knew that if Lila saw it, she was sure to buy it. "Lila," Jessica said, "when you go to the mall this afternoon, don't even bother looking in the Clothes Horse. I was in there the other day, and they didn't have anything interesting."

"OK, thanks," Lila said. "Tell your mother I hope she feels better. 'Bye."

Later that morning, Jessica went to the doctor's office with her mother. It seemed like Mrs. Wakefield was in the examining room for an eternity. With each passing minute, Jessica felt more and more edgy. *What could be taking so long?* Then Jessica had an awful thought: Maybe Dr. Costa was in there right now, breaking some bad news to her mother.

The more Jessica thought about it, the more sense it made. She glanced up at the clock behind the nurse's desk. Her mother had been in there for almost forty-five minutes! What was Dr. Costa telling her mother? That she had to go into the hospital? Or—Jessica's stomach tightened into a painful knot—something even worse?

Jessica couldn't stand waiting another second. She jumped up, determined to find out what was going on. But just then her mother walked into the waiting room. "Oh, Mom," Jessica cried, running to her side, "what happened? Are you going to be all right?"

"Of course I am," Mrs. Wakefield answered. "Dr. Costa gave me a thorough examination and took some more blood for testing, that's all." She looked closely at Jessica. "What's wrong, honey? You look upset."

"I am. I mean, I was." She gazed up into her mother's face. "It's just . . .oh, Mom, I was worried.

You were in there so long, I thought maybe Dr. Costa had found something really wrong with you."

Mrs. Wakefield put her arms around Jessica and hugged her tight. "It's nothing like that," she said reassuringly. I'll have the test results in a few days. Until then, he just wants me to stay in bed and rest."

Jessica leaned her head against her mother's shoulder. It felt good to be near her. Deep in the pit of her stomach, she still felt a little uneasy. But with her mother's arms around her, nothing seemed as horrible as she had imagined.

Mrs. Wakefield put her arms on Jessica's shoulders and looked at her. "I think you need something to get your mind off all this. In fact, we both do. Come on," she said, leading Jessica outside, "let's stop by the Dairi Burger on the way home. I feel in the mood for an ice cream soda."

"But I thought you were supposed to stay in bed for the next couple of days," Jessica said.

"That's all the more reason to go to the Dairi Burger." Mrs. Wakefield laughed. "This is my last chance to have a little fun for a while. Now, come on, what do you say?"

Jessica still felt a little uneasy. What if the test results showed that her mother had something seriously wrong with her? *Relax*, she told herself. She slipped her arm around her mother's waist. "An ice cream soda sounds great, Mom," she said with a smile.

Then Jessica remembered Elizabeth and Steven.

They were back home, vacuuming the house and mowing the lawn. Jessica felt a tiny stab of guilt. While they were working, she was going out for ice cream.

But Jessica quickly pushed the thought out of her mind. After all, there was nothing she could do to change things now. She might as well enjoy her soda. Still, just to make herself feel a little better, she said, "Mom, let's bring home some ice cream for Elizabeth and Steven, too."

Mrs. Wakefield smiled. "That's very thoughtful of you, Jessica. We will."

Mrs. Wakefield spent the next few days in bed. But instead of getting better, she seemed to get worse. She complained of feeling weak and achy, and had a sore throat and a slight fever.

On Monday afternoon, Jessica came home from school and told her brother and sister, "Tonight we're having pork chops, mashed potatoes, and peas for dinner. Steven, I'm putting you in charge of the pork chops."

"Gee, thanks a heap," he said sarcastically. "And I put you in charge of being a royal pain in the neck."

"Very funny," Jessica said, "but while we're joking around, Mom is upstairs, barely well enough to get out of bed."

"I know, but—"

"I'll make the mashed potatoes," Elizabeth volunteered.

"And I'll make the peas," Jessica finished.

"That isn't fair," Steven complained. "Throwing a package of frozen peas into a pot is no work at all."

"Steven's right." Elizabeth nodded. "Jessica, how about setting the table, too?"

"I don't have time," Jessica said quickly. "I have to make a cup of tea for Mom." Turning her back on her brother and sister, she walked to the stove to put on the kettle.

Mrs. Wakefield insisted on coming downstairs to eat dinner with the children that evening. When the meal was over, she sat back in her chair and sighed heavily. She looked pale and thin, and there were dark circles under her eyes.

Jessica looked at her mother across the table. *Every day Mom looks worse*, she thought anxiously. "You look tired, Mom," she said. "Do you want to go upstairs and lie down?"

"Not just yet," Mrs. Wakefield said. "I have something to tell all of you. First of all, I want to thank all three of you for the wonderful work you've been doing around the house. I'm so proud of you." Then she glanced at Jessica. "And I want to especially thank Jessica for taking such good care of me. She's been by my side every moment, fluffing my pillows, bringing me magazines, getting me drinks. A professional nurse couldn't have done better!"

Jessica saw Elizabeth and Steven exchange a look of disgust. Ignoring her brother and sister, she smiled proudly and said, "Thanks, Mom."

"Now, the big news," Mrs. Wakefield continued. "Dr. Costa called this morning to tell me the results of my test."

"What did he say?" Jessica asked, nibbling nervously on her thumbnail.

"Well, it was inconclusive. That means they still aren't sure what's wrong with me. But they do have a couple of ideas. There's a possibility I might have Epstein-Barr virus."

"Is that serious?" Steven asked.

"Not really," Mrs. Wakefield replied. "The treatment is just rest, rest, and more rest. And after a while it goes away by itself."

"That's good news," Elizabeth said with a relieved smile.

But Jessica wasn't so easily reassured. "What are the other possibilities?" she asked.

"Oh, some other type of virus, perhaps."

"But what if it's something serious?" Jessica insisted. She looked closely at her mother. She was almost positive she saw a worried look in her eyes. "It could be, couldn't it?"

"Well . . . all right. I'll be honest with you," Mrs. Wakefield said. "I think you're all grown-up enough to understand. Besides, I'd rather tell you the truth than lie and let you imagine all sorts of awful things." She took a deep breath. "The lump on my neck may be more serious. There's a very tiny chance it may be cancerous."

"Oh, Mom!" Jessica gasped. "Cancer!"

"Now, I don't want any of you to worry," Mrs.

Wakefield said quickly. "It's very, very unlikely that I have anything more serious than a virus. I'm going back to Dr. Costa tomorrow to have a biopsy done. He'll remove a tiny piece of the lump and look at it under a microscope. Then we'll know once and for all what's really wrong."

Jessica felt shaky all over. Her dinner was churning in her stomach, and her heart was pounding. "Maybe we should call Daddy," she suggested. She longed to hear her father's comforting voice. *He'll know what to do*, she thought.

"It's too late to call tonight," her mother answered. "Remember, it's three hours later in New York. I'll phone him tomorrow and let him know what's happening."

"And then he'll come home?" Jessica asked hopefully.

"There's no need for that—not unless the biopsy shows something more serious. But there's almost no chance of that happening."

"I hope you're right," Jessica said. But deep down, she had a frightening feeling her mother was very, very wrong.

That night, Jessica lay in bed, unable to fall asleep. Over and over again, she kept hearing the words her mother had said at dinner: *There's a very tiny chance it may be cancerous*. Jessica swallowed hard. If her mother was really sick, she might be sick for months and months. She might even die!

A wave of fear washed over Jessica. She tried to

imagine life without her mother. Who would she talk to when she had a problem? Who would love her? She felt so awful that she forgot all about the rest of the family. She imagined herself all alone in the world—a poor, motherless child.

A tear slid down Jessica's cheek and onto her pillow. She felt sure she was right. Her mother was dying. Soon she would be all alone. Jessica pressed her face into her pillow and sobbed. Finally, when she was too weak and exhausted to cry any more, she drifted off into a restless sleep.

Six

◇

When the alarm went off the next morning, Jessica woke up feeling tired and anxious. She sat up in bed and rubbed her eyes. The sun was shining brightly through the window, but Jessica's thoughts were as dark and gloomy as thunderclouds.

"Jess, are you awake?" It was Elizabeth. She opened the door and stuck her head in the room. "I've got a great idea. Let's surprise Mom by serving her breakfast in bed."

"Lizzie," Jessica said seriously, "come here."

Elizabeth walked into the room and sat down on the edge of the bed. "What is it?"

"Mom is very, very sick," Jessica announced solemnly. "I think"—her voice caught in her throat —"she's dying."

"What?" Elizabeth asked anxiously. "Who told you that?"

"She must be. Dr. Costa doesn't know what's wrong with her. And she said herself it might be cancer." Just saying the word made Jessica's eyes fill with tears.

"Jess, don't be silly," Elizabeth scolded. "Didn't you hear what Mom said last night? The lump can be removed. And besides, it's probably just a virus."

"I'm *not* being silly," Jessica insisted. "Mom is sick, and no one knows what's wrong with her. It's got to be something serious." She reached out and clutched her sister's hand. "Lizzie, I'm scared. Aren't you?"

Elizabeth sighed. "Yes," she admitted, "I am, a little. But there's no point in getting all worked up until we know all the facts."

"I know. You're right, But still . . . " Jessica wiped a tear from the corner of her eye.

"Don't cry, Jess," Elizabeth said gently. "Everything's going to be all right. I just know it is." She put her arm around her twin's shoulder and added, "Listen, you don't have to get up yet. Stay in bed, and I'll make breakfast for Mom *and* you."

Jessica smiled through her tears. Right then she wanted to be taken care of. After the horrible night she'd had, she felt she deserved it. "Thanks, Lizzie," she said, smiling weakly. "You're the best."

Later that morning, Jessica was in cooking class, learning how to make mashed potatoes. She and Lila were partners. They stood together over the stove, watching the potatoes boil.

But Jessica wasn't thinking about potatoes. Her mother's biopsy was scheduled for ten o'clock that morning. One of Mrs. Wakefield's friends from work was driving her to the doctor's office. Jessica glanced up at the clock. It was almost ten o'clock.

"The *Carnival* auditions are this Friday," Lila said. "Have you been practicing your audition song?"

"Huh?" Jessica replied absentmindedly.

"Your audition song," Lila insisted. "Have you practiced it? You're going to have to sing awfully well to beat out Dana Larson."

Lila was right, but Jessica couldn't think about that—not until she knew if her mother was going to be all right. "Uh, I've been kind of busy lately," she said.

"Oh, I almost forgot. Your mother. Did you find out what's wrong with her?"

"No, not yet."

"Gee, that's too bad," Lila said sympathetically. "I hope she feels better soon." She paused to turn down the heat under the potatoes. "Too bad you couldn't come shopping with us last Saturday. Valley Fashions got in a whole new batch of jeans. I bought three pairs."

Lila was still talking, but Jessica couldn't concentrate. *Please let Mom be OK*, she thought as she stared into the boiling water. *Please, please, please.* She repeated the words over and over in her head. But no matter how hard she wished, she couldn't get rid of the horrible sinking feeling in her stomach.

"All right, class," Mrs. Gerhart, the cooking instructor, told the class. "The next step is to put the cooked potatoes into the bowl with the milk and butter."

Jessica watched Lila dump the potatoes into their bowl, but her mind was wandering. *How long would it take to get the biopsy results?* she wondered. *Last time the test had taken two days. How can I live through two more days without knowing?* she thought miserably.

"Pick up your electric mixer, and lower the beaters into the bowl," Mrs. Gerhart was saying. "Now turn the mixer on very slowly."

Jessica turned on her mixer and thrust it into the bowl of mashed potatoes. To her horror, potatoes, milk, and butter flew out of the bowl and landed all over the counter. "No!" she cried, leaping back. The bowl overturned on the table and the mixer fell to the floor with a crash.

"Jessica Wakefield!" Mrs. Gerhart yelled. "Didn't you hear me tell you to put the mixer in the bowl *before* you turn it on?" She pointed at Jessica. "Class, now you know what happens if you try to put a spinning electric beater into a bowl of potatoes."

Everyone burst out laughing. Lila had gotten some potatoes on her sleeve, but even she was giggling. Jessica tried to smile, but her cheeks were hot with embarrassment. She felt humiliated, angry, and confused, all at the same time.

How can Mrs. Gerhart expect me to concentrate on a stupid thing like mashed potatoes at a time like this? she thought with frustration.

When Jessica got home that afternoon, she rushed to her mother's room. Mrs. Wakefield was lying in bed, reading a magazine. Jessica sat on the edge of the bed and took her mother's hand. "How was the biopsy?" she asked nervously.

"It was fine," her mother answered with a smile. "Dr. Costa said he'll call me with the results on Friday."

Jessica looked closely at her mother. She looked tired and weak. Her cheeks were sunken, and her normally tanned skin was pale. *Maybe she really is dying*, Jessica thought suddenly. "Oh, Mom," she cried, her voice catching in her throat, "I love you so much!"

"Jessica," Mrs. Wakefield said with surprise, "what's wrong?" She slipped her arms around Jessica and gave her a hug.

"I . . . I don't want you to die," Jessica sniffled into her mother's shoulder.

"Poor Jess," Mrs. Wakefield said gently. "All that talk about cancer scared you, didn't it?"

Jessica nodded silently.

"Sweetheart, I'm not going to die." Mrs. Wakefield sighed. "Believe me, everything's going to be fine. You'll see."

Jessica wanted to believe her mother, but deep inside, she still wasn't convinced.

"Come on," Mrs. Wakefield said, "let's see a smile. Tell me, are you still saving your money to buy the unicorn sweater you saw at the mall?"

The previous week the unicorn sweater had seemed like the most important thing in the world. But since her mother had gotten ill, Jessica had forgotten all about it. She sighed. "I don't know. I suppose so."

"You've been such a help around here these last few days," Mrs. Wakefield said. "Maybe it's too much to expect you to think about saving money right now. When I'm feeling better, you and I will go to the mall and buy you that sweater. Would you like that?"

"Sure, Mom," Jessica said, forcing herself to smile. "That would be great." But she couldn't help wondering if her mother would ever be well enough to go shopping again. "Are you going to call Daddy this afternoon?" she asked.

"Yes. As soon as Elizabeth and Steven get home."

"I'll bet when he hears how sick you are, he'll come right home," Jessica said hopefully.

"There's no reason for him to do that. And, Jessica, please," she added firmly, "I don't want you to say anything that might upset your father. He's working on an important case, and there's no reason for him to be worrying about us. Understand?"

Jessica nodded reluctantly. "I understand."

When Elizabeth and Steven got home, their

mother called Mr. Wakefield's hotel in New York.
"Hello, Ned," she said cheerily when the call had
been put through. "How are you?" A few minutes
later she calmly told her husband about the lump on
the back of her neck and the tests Dr. Costa had
done.

Jessica listened anxiously. Suddenly, she had a
horrible thought. What if something happened to
her mother before her father got home?

"No, no, everything's fine," Mrs. Wakefield was
saying. "Dr. Costa is almost certain it's a virus." She
paused. "Yes, I'll call you as soon as I get the results.
OK, Ned, I'll put the kids on."

Jessica listened while Elizabeth and Steven took
their turns talking to their father on the phone. Both
of them talked cheerfully about things that were happening at school. Then it was Jessica's turn.

"Hi, sweetie," her father said. "How's my girl?"

Jessica's knees felt weak. *Come home, Daddy*, she
longed to cry. *I'm scared*. But then she remembered
her mother's warning: *I don't want you to say anything
that might upset your father*. "Uh . . . I'm fine, Daddy,"
she managed to whisper.

"How's school? Anything new?"

"No . . . not really."

"Is everything all right, Jessica?" Mr. Wakefield
asked. "You sound awfully quiet."

"I . . . I'm OK."

"Good. Well, put your mother on again, will
you?"

Jessica handed the phone back to her mother. It had taken all her strength to hide her fears from her father, and now she felt shaky and weak.

After dinner that night, Jessica went down to the basement to practice her ballet. But she couldn't seem to concentrate on her warm-up routines. Instead, she put on a tape of Tchaikovsky's *Swan Lake*. The melancholy music suited her mood.

When the music ended, Jessica turned off the tape and went upstairs. As she reached the top step, the phone started ringing. She walked into the den and answered it.

"Hi," a girl's voice said. "Is this Jessica or Elizabeth?"

"This is Jessica," she said. "Who's this?"

"Caroline Pearce. Is Elizabeth there? I need to talk to her about our meeting tomorrow."

Jessica could hear someone coughing upstairs. Was it her mother? Jessica frowned. It was the first time she had heard her mother cough since she'd gotten sick. A shudder of fear went through her. *Is Mom getting worse?* she wondered anxiously.

"Jessica," Caroline said in her prissiest voice, "may I *please* talk to Elizabeth?"

"I can't talk right now," Jessica said seriously, "and neither can Elizabeth. Our mother is sick."

"She is?" Caroline asked curiously. "What's wrong with her?"

"We're not sure yet. Listen, I have to go."

"You sound upset," Caroline persisted. "It's nothing serious, is it?"

"It might be. But—"

"Oh, poor Jessica!" Caroline cooed sympathetically. "You must be so upset!"

All day long Jessica had been trying to hide her feelings—first in school, then on the phone with her father. Now she was too tired and too unhappy to try anymore. "I *am* upset," she admitted. "My mother is sick—very sick. No one knows what's wrong with her. It's scary."

"Oh, no!" Caroline gasped.

Jessica heard her mother cough again, louder this time. "Listen, I have to hang up. My mother needs me."

"Of course, Jessica. I understand."

Jessica hung up the phone and hurried upstairs. By the time she reached her mother's room, she had forgotten all about Caroline's call.

Seven

◇

Early the next morning, Elizabeth was sitting on the front steps of the school, waiting for Caroline Pearce. The day before, the girls had agreed to meet before school to discuss Caroline's latest gossip column for *The Sweet Valley Sixers*.

The minutes ticked by, but Caroline didn't show up. Finally, Elizabeth saw her friend, Amy Sutton, ride up on her bike. Aside from Jessica, Amy was her closest friend. They always sat together at lunch, and they worked together on *The Sweet Valley Sixers*. "Amy," Elizabeth called, "hi!"

"What are you doing here?" Amy asked in surprise.

"Waiting for Caroline Pearce. We were supposed

to meet to talk about her latest gossip column, but she didn't show up. Get this—Caroline wrote that Ms. Luster is marrying an Italian count and moving to Rome!" Elizabeth laughed, trying to imagine their school librarian falling in love with an Italian count. "I don't want to print something that nutty unless Caroline can prove it's true."

But Amy wasn't laughing. "I didn't expect to see you in school today," she said. "I thought you'd be home with your mother."

"Huh? What do you mean?"

"Caroline called me last night and told me about your mom." Amy reached out and took Elizabeth's hand in hers. "Oh, Elizabeth, I'm so sorry."

Elizabeth felt completely confused. "What are you talking about? What did Caroline tell you about my mother?"

"That she's sick, and no one knows what's wrong with her. That . . . that she's dying. She said she called your house last night, and Jessica told her all about it."

Now Elizabeth felt worried. *Does Jessica know something I don't?* she wondered. "Listen, Amy, I've got to find Jessica. I'll talk to you later, OK?"

By now the lawn in front of the middle school was crowded with students. Elizabeth hurried through the crowd, searching for her twin.

Olivia Davidson, the president of the student council, was standing by the flagpole, talking with some friends. "I'm sorry about your mother," she said as Elizabeth passed by. "You must be so upset."

"Is there anything we can do?" Sophia Rizzo asked.

Elizabeth could hardly believe her ears. Did the whole school know her mother was sick? "How did you hear about my mom?" she asked.

"Caroline Pearce told us," Olivia said.

"Is it true your mother has leukemia?" Jennifer Norris asked.

"I thought it was pneumonia," Sophia said.

"Leukemia? Pneumonia!" Elizabeth cried. "What are you talking about? It's probably just a bad virus, that's all."

"Of course it is," Sophia said, patting her on the back.

Elizabeth could tell that no one believed her. Suddenly she felt worried again. Maybe her mother really *was* dying. "Have you seen my sister?" she asked.

"Maybe she's over by the fountain," Olivia suggested. "I saw some of the other Unicorns over there."

Elizabeth hurried across the lawn. On the way, she noticed Caroline Pearce whispering something to Dennis Cookman and Winston Egbert.

"Caroline," Elizabeth said, stepping up beside her, "you were supposed to meet me on the front steps of the school fifteen minutes ago. Why didn't you show up?"

Caroline looked surprised. She clutched her

books to her chest and pushed a strand of red hair from her cheek. "Elizabeth, I didn't expect to see you in school today. After what Jessica told me . . ."

"Just what *did* Jessica tell you?"

"That your mother is very, very sick." She lowered her voice to a near-whisper. "You can tell me, Elizabeth. Is she really going to die?"

The word sent a shiver through Elizabeth. She just couldn't believe it was true. And even if it was, what right did Caroline have to tell the whole school?

"Listen, Caroline," Elizabeth said sternly, "our mother is sick, but it's probably nothing more serious than a virus. So just stop blabbing to everyone that she's dying, OK?"

"*Well,*" Caroline said in a huffy voice, "I don't know why you're mad at *me*. I just repeated what Jessica told me."

"That my mother has leukemia? Or pneumonia? I can't believe Jessica told you *that!*"

"Pardon me," Caroline said primly. "I just thought you'd appreciate a little sympathy from your friends, that's all."

There was an uncomfortable silence. Then Caroline asked, "What did you want to see me about this morning, anyway?"

Elizabeth shook her head. Right now she had too much on her mind to care if Ms. Luster was marrying an Italian count or not. "It's not important," she said as she walked away.

Elizabeth walked toward the fountain. But before she got there, she saw Jessica riding up the sidewalk on her bicycle. "Jessica, wait up!" Elizabeth cried, hurrying over to meet her.

"Hi, Lizzie," Jessica said as she hopped off her bike. "What's up?"

"Why did you tell Caroline Pearce that Mom is dying?" Elizabeth asked urgently. "Did you find out something I don't know?"

Jessica's mouth fell open. "*Dying*! I never said that!"

"Well, what *did* you tell her?"

"I can hardly remember. Let's see . . . I guess I told her that Mom is sick. And that we're not sure what's wrong with her."

"Jessica, how could you? You know how Caroline loves to stretch the truth. Homeroom hasn't even started yet, and she's already told half the school that Mom's dying!"

Jessica gasped. She felt shocked and embarrassed. But at the same time, she couldn't help feeling just a tiny bit pleased. Over the last few days she'd been so worried about her mother she could hardly stand it. Why shouldn't she be allowed to share her grief with her friends?

"Jessica!" someone cried from across the lawn. "Oh, you poor thing!"

Jessica and Elizabeth looked up to see Ellen Riteman walking toward them. Ellen threw her arms around Jessica and gave her a hug. "Caroline told me about your mother," she said with a pained look on her face. "Jess, why didn't you tell me?"

Jessica could feel Elizabeth looking at her. She knew her twin expected her to say that their mother wasn't really dying. But Jessica didn't want to. "I don't know, Ellen," she answered with a shrug. "I guess I just didn't want to bother you with my problems."

"Oh, Jess," Ellen said admiringly, "you're so brave!"

Elizabeth stared at Jessica in disbelief. But before she could say anything, the school bell rang.

"I'll talk to you at lunch," Ellen said, giving Jessica's arm a squeeze. "Hang in there. You, too, Elizabeth." Then she turned and hurried into the school.

"How could you, Jess?" Elizabeth demanded when Ellen had left. "How could you just stand there and let Ellen think our mother is at death's door?"

"Because it's true," Jessica cried.

Elizabeth opened her mouth to protest, but Jessica cut her off. "Oh, Lizzie, I know you don't think so, but I do. Mom's getting weaker and weaker. It's just a matter of time before we find out the truth. I'm scared, Lizzie," she said, her voice trembling. "I don't want Mom to die."

Elizabeth sighed. How could she be angry? Jessica was worried about their mother, and Elizabeth couldn't blame her for that. After all, she was worried, too. "It's all right, Jess," she said gently. "Everything's going to turn out fine." She smiled and added. "Now come on, let's get inside before

Mr. Clark catches us out here and gives us detention."

Jessica tried to laugh, but all she could manage was a weak smile. "OK, Lizzie." She slipped her arm around Elizabeth's waist, and together the twins walked up the steps to the school.

At lunch, Jessica joined the Unicorns at their favorite table. As soon as she sat down, everyone stopped talking and turned to her.

"How are you?" Lila asked with a concerned frown.

"Is there anything we can do for you?" Mary Wallace asked.

"Here, have one of the chocolate brownies I brought for lunch," Tamara Chase said. "I baked them last night."

"Thanks," Jessica said gratefully. After all the worrying she'd been doing lately, it felt good to be taken care of. Besides, she loved being the center of attention, even if the reason for all the attention was an unhappy one.

Finally, after everyone had said something nice to Jessica, the conversation turned to boys.

"Did you hear about Winston Egbert?" Janet asked. "Betsy Gordon overheard him telling Ms. McDonald that he wants to try out for *Carnival*."

Winston was a tall, quiet boy. Jessica thought he was weird because he practically never said a word, and whenever he was embarrassed his ears turned red.

"Can he sing?" Mary asked.

"Who knows?" Janet laughed. "And who cares?"

All the girls giggled. Jessica laughed, too, but her mind was far away. During the last few days she had barely given the school musical a moment's thought. She bit her lip thoughtfully. She wanted desperately to try out. But how could she find time to practice her audition song when she was so worried about her mother?

Besides, what if she got the part? How could she go to rehearsals and sing and dance as if she hadn't a care in the world? No, it just wouldn't be possible. She'd probably get up on stage and burst into tears.

"Are you still going to try out for the show, Jessica?" Ellen asked.

"I . . . I don't know," Jessica said. "I don't feel much like singing these days."

"But you would be a perfect Lily," Janet insisted.

"I think you should try out anyway," Lila said, leaning forward and smiling at Jessica. "You can't spend every single minute taking care of your mother. It's just to much to expect of yourself."

"Lila's right," Mary agreed. "Worrying about your mother can really get you down. But moping around the house isn't the answer. You have to get out and *do* something."

"I don't know," Jessica said tentatively. "Maybe you're right."

"Of course she is," Ellen said. "Besides, we

don't want Dana Larson to get the part. We want one of our friends to be the star of the show."

Jessica didn't know what to say. She didn't want to let the Unicorns down. And after all, she really did want to get the lead. Still, she had more important things to think about now. She shrugged. "I'll think about it," was all she said.

Eight

◇

That evening, the twins and Steven ate dinner upstairs in their parents' bedroom. "This is fun," Elizabeth said, sitting cross-legged on the bed with her plate of food in front of her. "Like a picnic."

"But without the bugs," Steven added, stuffing a handful of potato chips in his mouth.

Mrs. Wakefield took a sip of iced tea. "I talked to your father this morning," she said.

"Is he coming home?" Jessica asked hopefully.

"Soon. He's got a little more work to do, so I told him to stay. I'll call him Friday after I get the results of the biopsy." She took a bite of her hamburger. "This is delicious!" she exclaimed. "Better watch out, kids. You're becoming such good cooks, I might just let you keep the job—even after I get better!"

Elizabeth and Steven laughed, but Jessica could only manage a weak smile.

When dinner ended, the twins and Steven gathered the plates to take downstairs. In the hallway, Jessica turned to her brother and sister. "Steven, you can load the dishwasher. Elizabeth, I want you to wash the pans."

"And what are you going to do?" Steven demanded.

"Wipe off the counters," she replied.

"That's all?" Elizabeth asked with surprise.

Jessica looked hurt. "No, that's not all. I'm going to take Mom a dish of ice cream."

"I've had it!" Steven cried. "Ever since Mom got sick, you've been pushing Elizabeth and me around. Mom," he demanded, walking back into his mother's bedroom, "tell Jessica to stop acting like a dictator!"

Mrs. Wakefield was lying back against the pillow with her eyes closed. Her hair was mussed and her face looked as pale as the white pillowcase. Slowly her eyes fluttered open. "What's wrong, Steven?" she asked wearily.

"Nothing, Mom," Elizabeth said, stepping into the room and grabbing Steven's arm. "Sorry we bothered you. We're just fooling around." She gave him a sharp look. "Aren't we, Steven?"

"Uh . . . sure," Steven said. "Sorry, Mom. You just close your eyes and relax."

"There," Jessica said as Steven and Elizabeth

walked back into the hall, "I hope you're satisfied. We're supposed to be taking care of Mom, not upsetting her."

"OK, OK," Steven muttered. "I'll keep my mouth shut. But I still think you're being a royal pain."

"Come on," Elizabeth said generously, "I'll give you a hand with the dishes." Together they walked past Jessica and went downstairs.

After Jessica got the ice cream for her mother, she went to her room and started her homework. But her mind kept wandering to the *Carnival* auditions. Should she try out for the lead or shouldn't she?

Finally, Jessica got up from her desk and walked down the hall to her parents' room. Opening the door, she peeked inside. Her mother was sitting up in bed, reading a magazine.

"Come on in," Mrs. Wakefield said with a smile. She looked small and frail in the big double bed, and Jessica's heart ached.

"How are you feeling, Mom?" she asked.

"Oh, not too bad," Mrs. Wakefield said lightly. "But I feel as if I could sleep for about six years!" She took a sip of water from the glass on her night table. "And how are you, honey? Anything new at school?"

She shrugged. "The *Carnival* auditions are this Friday."

Mrs. Wakefield smiled. "I bet you're excited. Have you been practicing your audition song?"

"No, not really." She sighed. "I don't even know if I should try out. If I get the part, I'll have to go to rehearsals practically every day after school for weeks and weeks."

"Well, that's no problem—unless it interferes with your schoolwork, of course. How are your grades these days?"

Jessica thought about her unfinished homework, but she didn't want to worry her mother by mentioning it. "I'm doing fine, Mom," she said.

"Well, then, I don't see any reason why you shouldn't try out for the play."

"But, Mom," Jessica said, "what if you're still sick? I don't want to go to rehearsals if you need me at home."

"Don't be silly," Mrs. Wakefield replied, giving her daughter's arm an affectionate pat. "I'm going to be all better before you know it. Besides, you've been spending too much time worrying about me. You need to get involved in something fun. A role in the school play would be perfect."

"Well," Jessica began, "maybe . . ."

"Remember what I said when you first told me about the show?" Mrs. Wakefield asked.

Jessica nodded. "You said *Carnival* is one of your favorite musicals."

"That's right. In fact, I can still remember the first time I saw the movie. I was so excited that I ran right out and spent all my money to buy the soundtrack. I would dance around my house, pretending I was Lily and singing the songs over and over again. It drove my parents crazy!"

Jessica laughed, trying to picture her mother

dancing through the house, singing the songs from *Carnival*. She thought about the photographs she'd seen of her mother as a child.

"You know, I think you would make a perfectly lovely Lily," Mrs. Wakefield said.

"Oh, Mom, do you really think so?"

"Absolutely." She reached for Jessica's hand. "And it would make me so happy to see you up on that stage playing the lead."

Jessica nodded eagerly. Now that she knew how much the show meant to her mother, she had to try out for the lead. And not just try out—she had to get that part. She leaned over and gave her mother a kiss. "Don't worry, Mom. You'll see me up on that stage. I promise."

Mrs. Wakefield smiled. "Good. But if you're going to get that role, you'd better start practicing your audition song. Remember, the star of a musical has to sing her heart out."

"You're right, Mom," Jessica agreed, jumping up. "I will."

Jessica hurried out of the bedroom. As she walked down the hallway, she heard the sound of running water coming from downstairs. Elizabeth and Steven were in the kitchen, washing the dishes. Jessica paused at the top of the stairs. *Maybe I should go down and help them*, she thought.

Ignoring the guilty feeling that was creeping up inside her, Jessica ran into her room instead, and started to practice her song. After all, she couldn't let her mother down.

Jessica spent the rest of the evening in her room, singing "Look at Me." Finally, when her throat was too dry to sing another note, she went down to the kitchen for a drink. While she was pouring herself some soda, she noticed the take-out menu for Guido's Pizza Palace that Mrs. Wakefield kept taped to the refrigerator door. Jessica's stomach growled hungrily. A hot, gooey pizza would be just the thing to cheer her up. And after all the practicing she'd done, she deserved it.

According to the menu, a small cheese pizza cost three dollars and fifty cents plus fifty cents to have it delivered to the house. Jessica ran up to her room and checked her bank. All she had was three dollars.

Then she had an idea. Her parents always kept a few dollars around for small emergencies. The money was in the cookie jar on the shelf above the sink. She could borrow four dollars from the cookie jar and no one would even notice She would pay it back as soon as she got her allowance.

Jessica went back to the kitchen and opened the cookie jar. Inside were five one-dollar bills. *Great!* she thought. She could use the extra dollar to get pepperoni and extra cheese.

Jessica's stomach growled just thinking about it. Quickly, she took the money out of the cookie jar and picked up the phone to order the pizza

The next morning before school, Jessica met her friends at the fountain. "I've decided to go to the

Carnival auditions tomorrow," she told them. "My mother wants me to try out, and I don't want to let her down. It would mean so much to her to see me up on that stage before . . ." Her voice trailed off.

"Oh, Jess, you're so brave!" Lila breathed, squeezing Jessica's hand.

"I know you'll get the part," Janet said. "You just *have* to!"

"After all you've been through, you deserve it," Tamara added.

Jessica shrugged modestly. But inside, she couldn't help feeling Tamara was right. Since her mother had become sick, Jessica's life had been just awful. Winning the lead in the musical wouldn't make up for all the sadness, but it might cheer her up just a little bit. *Besides*, she thought, *it would mean so much to Mom.*

By lunch time, the whole school had heard that Jessica was auditioning for the musical to please her dying mother.

"Good luck, Jessica," Olivia Davidson said as they waited in the lunch line. "I hope you get the part."

"Me, too," Sophia Rizzo said.

Even kids Jessica barely knew came up to her during lunch to wish her luck. Tim Davis, one of the stars of the basketball team, walked by the Unicorn table and said, "Good luck, Jessica." And Virginia Walker, the secretary of the student council, said, "I sure hope you get the part."

Later, as Jessica left the cafeteria, she noticed

Tom McKay, Winston Egbert, and Ken Matthews sitting at a table by the door. "Hey, star," Tom called, "how about giving us your autograph?"

Jessica pretended she hadn't heard him, but inside she was smiling. It seemed that everyone in the whole school wanted her to get the lead. *Like Tamara said*, Jessica told herself, *I deserve it*.

Nine

◇

On Friday morning, Elizabeth got up early and walked outside to her "thinking seat"—a low branch on the huge pine tree in the backyard where she went when she wanted to be alone. Resting her head against the tree trunk, she breathed in the sweet smell of the sap. *Today we'll find out what's wrong with Mom*, she thought.

Elizabeth shook her head, trying to chase her deepest fears away. *It can't be true*, she told herself. *Jessica just gets carried away sometimes, that's all*. Still, she couldn't help feeling worried. "Oh, Mom," she whispered as her eyes filled with tears. "I don't want you to die."

A few minutes later, Elizabeth heard Jessica and Steven come downstairs. Quickly, she dried her eyes and went inside. "Good morning," she said, joining them at the kitchen table.

"Hey, Elizabeth," Steven said, pouring himself some cereal.

"Today we find out the truth," Jessica announced gloomily. She rested her chin on her hands and let out a long, mournful sigh.

"I wish you'd knock off the melodrama," Steven complained. "We're worried enough without you bringing us all down."

"I can't help it," Jessica answered. "I just keep thinking about how Mom used to be down here every morning, making breakfast for us. Now . . . well, maybe she never will be."

Elizabeth and Steven were silent for a moment. Jessica's gloomy outlook was making them feel gloomy, too.

Finally, Elizabeth broke the silence. "Poor Jessica," she said sympathetically. "You look almost as bad as Mom. You're pale, you've got circles under your eyes. . . ."

Jessica let out a ragged sigh. "What do you expect? It hasn't been easy keeping the house running smoothly *plus* taking care of Mom."

"Oh, brother," Steven muttered. "Give me a break!"

"Well, it's true!" Jessica snapped.

Elizabeth shook her head in disbelief. How could Jessica make a claim like that? Elizabeth and Steven had been the ones who had kept the house running smoothly, not Jessica. They had done all the cooking, all the cleaning, all the washing and ironing. Jessica's only job had been to give the orders and boss them around.

But Elizabeth kept silent. She knew that if she criticized Jessica it would only start a fight, and she didn't want that to happen while their mother was sick.

"I don't know how you're ever going to make it through school today, Jess. Why don't you just stay home?" Steven suggested.

"No," Jessica said. "I have to go to school. The *Carnival* auditions are this afternoon, and you know how much it would mean to Mom if I got the lead."

During the past two days, Jessica had practiced her audition song in every free moment. She had even found a copy of the *Carnival* script in the public library, and she had read it over and over. She knew the part of Lily inside out.

Elizabeth was glad her twin was trying out for the show. As far as she could see, it was the only thing that was keeping Jessica from falling apart completely. And no matter how annoyed Elizabeth felt about her sister's behavior, she never wanted to see Jessica unhappy. They were twins, and twins had to stick together.

Elizabeth reached across the table to squeeze her sister's hand. "Good luck this afternoon, Jess," she said. "I just know you're going to be terrific."

For the first time all morning, Jessica managed a smile. "Thanks, Lizzie," she said gratefully. "I just hope you're right."

"Good morning, class," Ms. Wyler said. "Please close your books and take out a piece of paper and a pencil. We are having a quiz."

"A quiz!" Amy Sutton cried. "You didn't tell us you were giving a quiz today!"

"No, I didn't," Ms. Wyler said calmly, "but if you were paying attention in class this week, you'll do just fine."

"But wait," Aaron Dallas interrupted. "Couldn't we review fractions just one more time? I mean, all that common denominator stuff is really confusing."

"No," Ms. Wyler replied. "You've had plenty of chances to ask questions. Now, I want all of you to keep quiet and get to work." She picked up a piece of chalk and began writing math problems on the board.

Everyone was taking out paper and pencils and setting to work. But Jessica was staring off into space, thinking about her mother. *Maybe at this very moment Dr. Costa was calling to let her know that she had cancer. Maybe he was telling her that she had only a few months to live.*

Tears welled up in Jessica's eyes and spilled over onto her cheeks. A few kids turned to stare at her, but she was too miserable even to care.

Finally, Ms. Wyler turned around. "Jessica," she began, "please get out a pencil and—" Then she noticed that Jessica was crying. "Would you like to go to the girls' room for the rest of the period?"

"Thank you," Jessica sniffled, barely able to hold

in her sobs. She gathered up her books and hurried from the room.

Ms. Wyler turned to Elizabeth. "You're excused, too, of course. Would you like to join your sister?"

"That's all right," Elizabeth said. She was upset, but standing around in the girls' room certainly wasn't going to make her feel any better. "I'd rather take the quiz." She picked up her pencil and set to work.

Meanwhile, in the girls' room, Jessica sat in one of the stalls and sobbed. Her whole world was falling apart. Her mother was dying, her father was thousands of miles away. The only thing she had to look forward to was her *Carnival* audition. Jessica took out her copy of the script and tried to study Lily's lines. *I've got to get that part*, she thought desperately. *For Mom's sake.* But her hands were trembling, and the page looked blurry through her tears. Finally, she gave up. With a mournful sob, she dropped the script and put her head in her hands. Then she cried until she just couldn't cry anymore.

At lunchtime, the twins met at the pay telephone in the school's front lobby. Elizabeth dropped a coin in the slot and dialed home. The moment she heard her mother's voice she asked anxiously, "Did the doctor call?"

Jessica stood beside her sister. She pressed her ear close to the receiver, straining to hear her mother's reply.

"Not yet," Mrs. Wakefield said. "Call back as soon as school ends. I'm sure I'll know by then. And don't worry, girls. No matter what happens, we'll handle it—together."

With a sigh, Elizabeth hung up the phone and looked at her sister. "Nothing yet."

Jessica felt frantic. "The waiting is making me crazy," she moaned. "I don't know how I'm going to make it through the afternoon."

"Try not to think about it," Elizabeth told her. "Just concentrate on your classes. It's the only way."

"I wish I could. But when your one and only mother is sick, school just doesn't seem that important."

Elizabeth nodded. Then she put her arms around Jessica's shoulder, and together the twins walked to the cafeteria.

The afternoon was absolute torture. The minutes dragged by, and every period seemed to last for hours. Both Jessica and Elizabeth were sick with worry. In less than three hours they would find out, once and for all, what was wrong with their mother.

Despite her fears, Elizabeth managed to sit through her classes. It wasn't easy to pay attention to Mr. Bowman's lecture on prepositional phrases or Mr. Nydick's questions on American history. Still, it helped keep her mind off her mother's illness.

But Jessica couldn't hold in her feelings the way Elizabeth could. She burst into tears in English class and again in science. Both times she was excused from class, and she spent the rest of each period in the lavatory, clutching her *Carnival* script to her chest and sobbing.

Then at last, the school day came to an end. Jessica left the lavatory and rushed to the lobby. At the same time Elizabeth was running out of history class and heading for the lobby too.

The twins met at the pay telephone. Jessica fumbled in her pocket for a coin. Jamming it into the phone, she dialed home. She and Elizabeth pressed their ears to the receiver, waiting breathlessly as the phone rang once . . . twice . . . three times.

"Hello?"

"Mom," Jessica cried, "what happened?"

"Good news!" Mrs. Wakefield exclaimed. "The lump isn't cancerous. Dr. Costa says I just have a very bad virus. It's going to take a few weeks of rest before I feel better, but it's not serious."

Jessica could hardly believe her ears. She dropped the receiver and let out a whoop of joy. "Mom's going to be all right!" she cried joyously. "She's not going to die!"

"Hurray!" Elizabeth exclaimed. "What a relief!"

The twins hugged each other tight. They were laughing and crying at the same time. Suddenly the whole world looked bright and beautiful. Everything was going to be fine!

Ten

◇

Jessica was so overjoyed she practically skipped down the hall. Now that she knew her mother was going to be fine, she was *really* looking forward to the *Carnival* auditions. She turned the corner and walked eagerly into the school auditorium. She could hardly wait to tell everyone the good news about her mother.

The lights were on inside the auditorium, and the curtain was up on the stage. A few dozen boys and girls were milling around the aisles, anxiously waiting for the auditions to begin. Jessica recognized Winston Egbert and Pamela Jacobson in the crowd. Then she noticed Bruce Patman. He was sitting off the aisle with his legs hooked over the seat in front of him. Jessica sighed, thinking how wonderful it would be to star with him in the show.

Ms. McDonald was sitting at the piano at the front of the auditorium, leafing through some sheet music. Jessica strolled down the aisle with an enormous grin on her face. She was feeling great. Her only worry was Dana Larson. Could Jessica win the lead away from her? It all depended on what Ms. McDonald thought was more important—singing or acting ability and good looks.

As Jessica passed Winston Egbert, he smiled shyly and said, "Hi, Jessica. How's your mom doing?"

Normally, Jessica didn't pay attention to a nerd like Winston. But today she wanted to tell absolutely everyone her good news. "Thanks for asking, Winston," she began. "I—"

"Excuse me, Jessica, can I talk to you?"

Jessica looked up to find Dana Larson standing beside her. Her short blond hair hung loosely around her face, and she was dressed casually in jeans and a T-shirt. Jessica frowned. *What could she want?* she wondered.

"Please," Dana said. "It's important."

Jessica followed Dana to a nearby seat. They sat down next to each other, and Jessica asked, "Well, what is it?"

"I've decided not to audition for the show," Dana said simply.

Jessica was stunned. "But—but why not?" she asked in disbelief.

"I want you to have the part of Lily," Dana explained. "I think you need it now more than I do."

Jessica opened her mouth, but she was so surprised she couldn't think of anything to say.

"Please, don't argue," Dana said. "I know you have your heart set on getting the part, and I want you to have it. Besides, my mother can see me act some other time. This might be your mother's last chance to see you."

Suddenly, Jessica realized what was going on. Dana thought Mrs. Wakefield was dying! That's why she was dropping out of the auditions and letting Jessica have the part!

At that moment, Ms. McDonald walked up the aisle to join them. "I guess Dana told you she's not trying out for the lead," she said to Jessica. "Dana and I talked it over, and we both agreed it was the right thing to do. In fact, just before you arrived I explained our decision to the other girls who were planning to audition for the role. They all agreed that you deserve to be Lily."

"You mean I don't even have to try out?" Jessica asked in amazement.

"No," Ms. McDonald said sympathetically. "If you want the part, it's yours."

Jessica's mind was racing. She knew why everyone was being so nice to her: It was because they felt sorry for her. But what if they knew her mother was OK? Then Ms. McDonald would probably go ahead with the auditions as planned. And if she did, there was a good chance Dana would get the part of Lily.

Jessica knew she should tell the truth. But something was stopping her. She wanted that part—wanted it more than anything. She could almost hear the deafening applause as the audience jumped to their feet to give her a standing ovation after the show.

It only took Jessica a moment to make up her mind. "Thank you, Dana," she said slowly. "I really appreciate what you're doing for me. I just hope I can return the favor someday."

Dana gave Jessica a quick hug. "I'm happy to do it. I only wish I could do something to help your mom get better."

"How is your mother doing?" Ms. McDonald asked with concern.

"Oh . . . uh, about the same," Jessica mumbled.

"Well, send her my best," she said. Then she turned to the rest of the students and announced, "Jessica Wakefield will play the part of Lily. Let's all give her a hand."

Everyone clapped loudly. Jessica could feel her cheeks turning red. She felt a little guilty, and for a moment she almost wished she had told the truth. But then she changed her mind, This was her big chance to be a star. She'd be an idiot to turn it down.

Besides, it wasn't as if she was lying, exactly. She was just keeping her mouth shut for a couple of days, that was all. On Monday she would tell everyone the real truth—that her mother wasn't going to die after all. But by then it would be too late for Ms. McDonald to give the part to Dana.

Everyone was still applauding. Jessica looked around the auditorium and smiled happily. She loved being the center of attention. "Thank you," she said, standing up and taking a bow. "Thank you very much!"

When Jessica got home, she found her whole family sitting in the living room—including her father!

"Daddy!" she cried happily, running up to give him a hug and a kiss. "I thought you weren't coming home until next week!"

"It didn't take as long to settle this case as I thought it would," he said. "So I packed my bags and caught an earlier flight. I just got here a few minutes ago." He put his arm around his wife. "Your mother's been telling me what a big help you kids were while I was away."

Mrs. Wakefield nodded. She still looked tired and weak, but she was smiling radiantly. "They've been running this house better than I do. And Jessica—what a nurse! She's been waiting on me hand and foot."

Jessica beamed with happiness. She loved it when her parents praised her. And she knew that when they heard her big news, they would praise her even more. "Guess what?" she announced. "I've got the lead in *Carnival*!"

"Jessica, that's wonderful!" her mother exclaimed.

"Hey, not bad," Steven said.

"I'm impressed," Elizabeth added. "You had some tough competition. Dana Larson has a super voice."

Jessica coughed nervously. She couldn't tell her family how she had really gotten the part.

"What terrific children we have!" Mr. Wakefield said. "All three of you deserve a medal. But I've got something almost as good." He left the room and came back with a large cardboard box. "Go on, open it."

Steven got to the box first and ripped it open. "Candy bars!" he exclaimed, pulling out a handful. "Hundreds of candy bars!"

"Compliments of the My-T-Good Chocolate Company," Mr. Wakefield said.

Steven was already gobbling down one of the candy bars. "Mmm, this is good!" he said between bites.

"Don't spoil your dinner," Mrs. Wakefield warned.

"That's right," Jessica said in her bossiest tone. "Tonight we're having meat loaf. Elizabeth, I want you to set the table, and Steven—"

"Hold on," Mr. Wakefield broke in. "You've all done more than your share of work lately. Tonight *I'm* cooking dinner!"

Everyone cheered.

"All this good news calls for a celebration," Mrs. Wakefield said happily. She looked around at her family. "We have a lot to be thankful for."

"Right," Mr. Wakefield said with a nod. "I'm

going to the supermarket right now to buy some cake and ice cream for dessert. Anyone want to come along?"

Elizabeth and Steven jumped to their feet. "Me!" they cried in unison.

But Jessica shook her head. "I think I'll stay home with Mom." she said. As the rest of the family got ready to leave for the store, she sat down on the sofa and gave her mother a big hug. "I'm glad you're going to be all better soon, Mom," she said. And she meant it with all her heart.

That night Jessica lay in bed and thought about her day. Almost everything she wanted had come true. Her mother wasn't going to die, and her father was home. Plus, she had gotten the lead in *Carnival*!

So why didn't she feel happy? Was it because she had lied about her mother's illness to get the part? No, she thought, there wasn't anything wrong with what she'd done. It was just a little white lie— hardly worth thinking about. And besides, her mother really *could* have been dying. In fact, up until three o'clock this afternoon, Jessica had been certain it was true.

Still, Jessica had an odd feeling in the pit of her stomach that just wouldn't go away. She took a deep breath and forced herself to ignore it. Then she rolled over, closed her eyes, and fell into an uneasy sleep.

Eleven

◇

On Saturday, Mr. Wakefield prepared breakfast. The family sat around the dining table, eating, talking, and laughing happily.

"Anything new at school, girls?" Mr. Wakefield asked.

Elizabeth looked up from her French toast. "Caroline Pearce wrote in her gossip column in the *Sixers* that the school librarian is marrying an Italian count and moving to Rome," she said.

"She *is*?" Jessica asked with interest.

"Nope," Elizabeth answered. "I finally got a chance to talk to Ms. Luster yesterday afternoon. She's going to Rome, all right, but it's just a vacation. Her brother lives there. He's a clerk in a big department store." She laughed. "I guess Caroline overheard Ms. Luster talking about him and thought she said 'count' instead of 'clerk'!"

Jessica giggled. "Caroline never gets anything right!"

"I know!" Elizabeth said, giving her twin a meaningful look. "That's why I never tell her anything personal about myself . . . *or* my family."

Jessica knew Elizabeth was still angry with her for telling Caroline that Mrs. Wakefield was ill. But Jessica didn't want to be reminded of that now. Ignoring Elizabeth, she turned to her mother. "Mom, remember that unicorn sweater I saw at the mall? Are you still going to buy it for me?"

"Of course I am," Mrs. Wakefield replied. "If you can wait a week or so until I'm feeling better, I'll take you to the mall and buy each of you something special. You deserve it for taking such good care of me."

That was exactly what Jessica wanted to hear, and it should have made her happy. But, no matter how hard she tried, she couldn't stop worrying about what had happened at the *Carnival* auditions. What if someone found out that she had lied to get the part? She'd not only be in terrible trouble, she'd also be the laughingstock of the whole middle school.

After breakfast, Mr. Wakefield suggested that they all go out for a swim. Elizabeth and Steven immediately dashed up to their bedrooms to get their bathing suits. But Jessica didn't want to go outside. What if someone from school came by and saw her laughing and splashing in the pool? That was hardly the way for someone with a dying mother to behave! "You go ahead," she said to her father. "I, uh . . . I have some homework to do."

Ten minutes later, Jessica heard the doorbell ring. She waited for someone else to answer it, but when the bell rang again, she got up and went downstairs. When she opened the front door, her stomach dropped. There on the porch were three of the girls who had been at the *Carnival* auditions— Brooke Dennis, Sandra Ferris, and Dana Larson!

"Wha—what are *you* doing here!" Jessica exclaimed.

"We just thought we'd come over and see how you're doing," Dana said with a kind smile.

"Oh, uh, thanks," Jessica stammered. She felt stunned—and horrified! Behind her she could hear the happy sounds of her family, shouting and splashing in the backyard pool. She tried to ignore them. "I'm okay, I guess," she said with a sigh.

"You should have stayed around after the auditions," Dana said. "Ms. McDonald announced the results. All three of us are in the show. I'm playing the leader of the carnival acrobats."

"Gee, that's great," Jessica said weakly.

"And Bruce Patman is going to be the magician," Brooke added, her eyes sparkling.

Jessica didn't know what to say. Her dream had come true. She was co-starring in the school musical with Bruce Patman. But right now she was much too nervous to enjoy her triumph. If Dana and her friends found out that Jessica had lied about her mother, everything would be ruined. Somehow she had to keep them away from her family—at least until Monday. But how?

Just then, Jessica heard Steven talking out on the patio. "I'm going inside to get a glass of lemonade," he called to the rest of the family. "Anybody else want one?"

"Sure," Mr. Wakefield answered.

Jessica thought fast. "Uh, my mother is sleeping, so we have to be quiet," she said. "Let's go into the den."

Quickly, she herded Dana, Brooke, and Sandra into the den—just seconds before Steven walked into the house.

Closing the door behind her, Jessica sat on the couch and heaved a sigh of relief. Now all she had to do was think of a way to get Dana and her friends out of the house before any of the Wakefields noticed they were there.

"You're going to be a wonderful Lily," Dana said, joining Jessica on the couch. "I'm really glad you decided to take the part."

Jessica wished Dana would be quiet. She felt guilty enough about what she'd done without having Dana act so incredibly sweet to her. "Thanks," she mumbled.

"It's the least I could do," Dana went on. "I just feel so bad about you mom. We all—"

Dana's last word was drowned out by the sound

of laughter coming from the kitchen. Jessica froze. A family with a dying mother wasn't supposed to sound so happy!

The other kids were obviously thinking the same thing. They looked at each other uncertainly. "Uh, how's your mother feeling?" Brooke asked.

Jessica forced her face into a sad expression. It wasn't easy, though. Now that she knew her mother was going to get well, she wanted to shout it from the rooftops. "She's, uh, very weak," she said.

There was an unhappy silence. Then Dana announced, "There's a new movie playing at the mall. We're all going this afternoon. Why don't you come with us, Jessica? It'll be our treat."

"Yes, please come," Sandra said encouragingly. "I'm sure it will cheer you up."

Jessica smiled with relief. She wanted nothing better than to get the girls as far away from her house as possible. But just then the laughter from the kitchen began again. It sounded to Jessica as if Elizabeth and Steven were playing some kind of game with their father. She heard running footsteps, then a shriek, then Mr. Wakefield's voice and more giggles.

"I guess your family must be kind of tense right now," Sandra said.

Jessica wanted to tell the truth. But if she did, she would lose her starring role in *Carnival*. "Yes," she said, sniffling dramatically. She lowered her head and pretended to wipe away a tear. It was only an act, but it reminded her how horrible she had felt last week when she thought her mother really *was* dying.

She thought back to all the nights she had spent lying awake in her bed, worrying. Just the memory of it made her stomach twist into a painful knot. A tear slid down her cheek, but this time she wasn't faking. With a sad sigh, she reached up and wiped it away.

"Poor Jessica," Dana said sympathetically. She pulled a tissue out of her bag and offered it to her.

Jessica shook her head. Suddenly, she didn't want to go on lying about her mother anymore. The last two weeks had been the most miserable of her entire life. She never wanted to feel that unhappy again. She didn't even want to pretend.

Jessica stood up and paced across the room. There was only one way out of her predicament. She had to tell the truth. She swallowed hard. This wasn't going to be easy. Once she told everyone her mother was going to get better, she would have to give up her part in *Carnival*. It was only fair.

Jessica took a deep breath. "Listen," she began, "I have something important to tell you. I—"

But before she could finish the sentence, the door to the den burst open. Elizabeth came running in, her bathing suit dripping wet. "Oh, Jess," she gasped. "Steven put a fake ice cube with a fly in it into Daddy's lemonade!" She giggled with delight. "You should have seen Dad's face when he saw it!"

The girls stared at Elizabeth in stunned silence.

Elizabeth stared back, wondering why everyone looked so serious. Then everyone—including Elizabeth—turned to Jessica with a look that clearly said, *What in the world is going on?*

Thinking fast, Jessica cleared her throat and turned to Dana. "Now that my mother is going to be all right," she announced, "I want you to audition for the lead in the musical."

"What?" Dana asked in amazement. "You mean your mother isn't dying?"

"That's what I've been trying to tell you ever since you walked in here," Jessica lied. "We all thought she was really sick, but now we've learned it's just a bad virus. The doctor says Mom's going to be better in a few weeks."

Jessica didn't bother to mention that she had found out about her mother right before the Friday afternoon *Carnival* auditions. Luckily, everyone was so surprised and happy to learn that Mrs. Wakefield wasn't dying that they didn't think to ask.

"Oh, Jessica," Brooke cried, "that's wonderful!"

"You must be so relieved!" Sandra exclaimed.

"We are," Jessica nodded. "So you see," she said to Dana, "I couldn't ask you to give up the chance for the part. Not now. Besides," she added, practically choking on the words, "you deserve the lead. You have such a beautiful voice."

"Gosh, thanks," Dana said gratefully. "But are you sure about this? I mean, I *did* drop out of the competition."

Jessica was tempted to hold Dana to her word.

But her conscience was bothering her too much to go through with it. "No, Dana," she said at last. "I'm going to talk to Ms. McDonald on Monday. You deserve to be Lily, and that's that."

Dana leaped to her feet and threw her arms around Jessica. "Wow, thanks!" she gushed.

"Hey, why don't you come to the movie with us anyway?" Brooke suggested. "It's supposed to be really funny."

Jessica shook her head. Right now she felt more like crying than laughing. "No, thanks," she said. "You go on without me. I want to be with my family this afternoon."

"We understand," Dana said, standing up to leave. "Well, so long, Jessica. 'Bye, Elizabeth."

Jessica followed the girls to the front door and watched them ride away on their bikes. She was still standing at the door when Elizabeth came up behind her.

"Pretty sneaky, Jessica," Elizabeth said.

Jessica spun around. "Huh? What are you talking about?"

"We found out right after school ended on Friday that Mom was going to be OK. But you didn't tell anyone at the audition, did you?"

Jessica smiled sheepishly. "Well . . . no, but—"

"*Jessica!*" Elizabeth scolded. "How could you lie like that?"

Guilty tears welled up in Jessica's eyes. "I . . . I wanted the part so much." She shrugged helplessly.

"But even so," she said quickly, "I was just about to tell Dana the truth when you walked in."

Elizabeth looked at her hard. "Honest?"

"Honest! I couldn't bear to go on pretending. These last two weeks have been awful for me. Just awful. I never want to feel that bad again." She sniffed and wiped her eyes with the back of her hand.

Elizabeth hated to see her twin so unhappy. Still, she couldn't help feeling angry. The last two weeks had been awful for her, too. But *she* hadn't used her mother's illness as an excuse for everything.

Then suddenly Elizabeth had an idea. "Do you still have that list of chores you wrote for us when Mom got sick?" she asked.

"Of course. In fact, I was planning to give you and Steven your weekend work assignments this afternoon."

Elizabeth shook her head. "This weekend, *I'm* handing out the work assignments. I expect you to do all your regular chores, plus the jobs Steven and I have been doing. The cooking, the cleaning, the washing—everything!"

Jessica stared at her twin in disbelief. "But Lizzie—" she began.

"No arguments, Jess. Besides, it's the least you can do after the way you've been ordering Steven and me around."

"I heard my name," Steven said, walking in

from the living room in his bathing suit and a T-shirt. "I guess you must be talking about what a great guy I am, huh?"

Elizabeth laughed. "Sort of. Jessica was just telling me that she's decided to do all our chores for this weekend. Isn't that nice of her?"

Steven looked from Jessica to Elizabeth and back again. "Something's up," he said finally. "But whatever it is, I'm all for it." He patted Jessica on the shoulder. "Thanks a lot, Jess, old pal. You can start by cleaning up my room."

Jessica let out a loud sigh. "OK, OK. I get the picture. But first I want to check on Mom. She might want some tea or—"

"Oh, no, you don't," Steven said, grabbing her arm so she couldn't walk away. "Elizabeth and I will take care of Mom this weekend." He pointed toward the stairs. "I want you to march upstairs and get to work on my room. Then you can report back to me for instructions on what to do next."

"Steven," Jessica moaned, "give me a break!"

"It's not much fun being bossed around, is it?" Elizabeth asked.

Jessica sighed. She knew she was trapped. Still, she couldn't complain—not really. She was just relieved that her mother was not dying. Compared to that, nothing else seemed all that awful—not even a weekend of boring chores.

Twelve

◇

Jessica spent the rest of the weekend working. She vacuumed the rugs, scrubbed the bathrooms, mowed the lawn, cooked all the meals, and washed the dishes. She even cleaned up her own messy room.

Mr. and Mrs. Wakefield were amazed. More than once they asked Jessica why she was working so hard. But she just shrugged and said, "I want to help out. That's all."

Finally, late Sunday afternoon, they came into the kitchen to find Jessica making dinner. "Jessica," Mr. Wakefield said. "I was planning to take you, your brother, and your sister out for pizza."

"Oh, but I want to cook," Jessica answered. She

turned to her mother. "Are you sure you should be out of bed?" she asked with concern.

"Yes, I'm all right," Mrs. Wakefield answered. "I'm feeling stronger every day. But what about you? You've been working nonstop all weekend. It's about time you took a rest, isn't it?"

"I'm fine, Mom," Jessica insisted. "Besides, you're not all better yet. And until you are, I want to help out."

"That's sweet of you," Mrs. Wakefield said, "but you don't have to do everything."

"Yes," Mr. Wakefield agreed. "You didn't have to mow the lawn. That's usually my job." He chuckled and added, "*I'm* not sick, you know."

"I don't mind," Jessica said. "I'm just so happy Mom is going to get better."

"Poor dear," Mrs. Wakefield said, giving her daughter a kiss on the top of her head, "you were really worried about me, weren't you?"

"Of course I was. I . . . I was afraid you were going to die." Just thinking about it made a lump come to her throat.

"I know," Mrs. Wakefield said gently, "but that's all in the past now. I'm going to be fine." She smiled. "And by the time I'm well I'm going to have the cleanest house in all of California—thanks to you."

Jessica shrugged. "I'm happy to do it." And the funny thing was, she meant it.

By Sunday night, Jessica couldn't help feeling a little sorry for herself. What a crummy weekend it had been. Not only had she been forced to take over all the chores that Elizabeth and Steven normally did, but she had given up the lead in the school musical as well.

Jessica sighed as she stacked the dishwasher. It made her sad to think she had lost her chance to be the star of the show. Instead, it was Dana Larson who was going to be up on that stage, singing and dancing with Bruce Patman. Dana Larson—she wasn't even a Unicorn!

As Jessica turned on the dishwasher, her father walked into the room. "That was a delicious dinner, honey," he said. "You're turning into quite a cook."

"Thanks," Jessica said, but her heart wasn't in it. She didn't want to be a cook. She wanted to be the star of *Carnival*.

Mr. Wakefield opened the refrigerator. "Hmmm," he said, "no milk. And we're low on orange juice and bread. I'd better go to the market." He looked at Jessica. "Want to come along?"

"Sure," Jessica said, eager to get out of the house before Elizabeth and Steven thought up more chores for her to do.

On the way out, Mr. Wakefield looked in his wallet. "I forgot to go to the bank this weekend," he said. "Well, we'll just have to raid the cookie jar."

Jessica's heart skipped a beat. She thought back to the evening she had treated herself to a pizza from Guido's Pizza Palace. She had borrowed the money from the cookie jar, and she had forgotten to pay it back. "Uh, I have some money up in my room," she said quickly. "I'll go get it."

But it was too late. Mr. Wakefield had already walked to the shelf above the sink and opened the cookie jar. "Empty!" He frowned. "I'm sure there was some money in here before I went to New York." He turned to Jessica. "Do you know what happened to it?"

Jessica knew it would be easy to say that her mother had used the money to buy food while her father was away. Or she could say that she had seen Elizabeth or Steven take the money.

But lying had already gotten her into trouble once that weekend. The way her luck was running, she'd probably get into deeper trouble if she tried again. Instead, she decided to tell the truth—almost.

"I took the money, Daddy," she said, "but I was planning to pay it back. It's just . . . well, I was planning to buy some really pretty flowers for Mom."

Mr. Wakefield's stern expression softened into a smile. "That was very nice of you, Jessica."

Jessica smiled back, hoping her father would be so pleased that he wouldn't make her pay the money back.

"But you know the money in the cookie jar is only for your mother and me to use for small emergencies," he continued. "I want you to pay back the money you took as soon as you get your allowance."

"But, Daddy—"

"No buts. I want you to replace that money. Understand?"

Jessica nodded. Thanks to her big mouth, she had to use all her money to buy her mother a bouquet of flowers *plus* use the next week's allowance to make up the money she had taken. She let out a sigh. It seemed nothing was going her way! But then she remembered that things weren't all bad. Her mother was OK, wasn't she?

Jessica smiled as she followed her father to the garage. The next day she was going to buy her mother the biggest, most beautiful bouquet of flowers she could find—even if it took every cent she owned.

When Jessica and her father returned from the supermarket, the phone was ringing. "I'll get it," Jessica said, putting the bag of groceries on the counter. Her father nodded and walked into the living room.

Jessica picked up the phone. "Hello?"

"Hello. This is Ms. McDonald from the Sweet Valley Middle School. Is Jessica Wakefield there?"

A feeling of panic shot through Jessica's stomach. Why was Ms. McDonald calling her at home? Had she found out that Jessica had lied to win the lead in the show? "Um, this is Jessica," she said in a small, frightened voice.

"Oh, hello. I just wanted to tell you that Dana called me this afternoon and told me your mother is going to be all right. I'm so happy for you, and so pleased that you want Dana to try out for the lead in the show. That's very admirable of you, Jessica. Very admirable."

Jessica felt so relieved she practically burst out laughing. "Thank you, Ms. McDonald," she said happily.

"When I found out about Jennifer Norris, I wanted to call you right away. You see, Jennifer just learned that her family is moving to Seattle. She was going to be one of the carnival performers, but now that she's moving we need a replacement. It's not a large part, but do you think you might be interested? It does require some dancing and a solo song."

Jessica could hardly believe her good luck. "Interested?" she exclaimed with delight. "I'd *love* to do it!"

"Perfect! Then it's settled. Well, I'll see you tomorrow afternoon at our first rehearsal. Goodbye, Jessica."

Jessica hung up the phone and let out a whoop of joy. Suddenly, it had been the most wonderful weekend of her entire life. First she had learned that her mother wasn't seriously ill. And now she had gotten a role in *Carnival*—a role that was going to show off her dancing to the entire school!

Jessica felt happier than she had in a long, long time. She pretended she was up on the middle school stage, dancing her solo. Spinning gracefully across the kitchen floor, she curtsied to her imaginary audience. Then she skipped into the living room to tell Elizabeth the good news.

Thirteen

◇

One morning, two weeks later, Jessica was riding her bicycle to school. As she pedaled, she glanced down at her outfit. She was wearing a denim skirt, purple knee socks, navy flats—and the beautiful pale violet unicorn sweater! The night before, her mother had finally felt well enough to take her to the Valley Mall and buy it for her. Jessica smiled. *Wait till the Unicorns see it,* she thought, pedaling as fast as she could.

When Jessica got to the school, she parked her bike and hurried to find her friends. Lila, Janet, and Ellen were standing under the flagpole. "Hi," Jessica said as she walked up to join them.

"Hi, Jess," Lila replied. Then she noticed the sweater. "Ooh, where did you get it?"

"It's so beautiful!" Janet shrieked. "I just have to have one!"

"I got it last night at the Clothes Horse," Jessica said. She put out her arms and spun around to show off the sweater. "It was the only one in the whole store."

"The only one?" Janet moaned. "Oh, Jessica, you're so lucky!"

"Can I borrow it sometime?" Ellen begged. "I'll lend you my silver necklace—the one you told me you like so much."

Jessica was tingling with happiness. "Maybe sometime," she said generously. "After I've worn it a few—"

"Come back here, shrimp!" a voice cried.

Jessica looked up to see Winston Egbert running straight at her. With a gasp, she jumped out of the way, just as Winston ran past. Dennis Cookman came next, chasing after him.

"Watch where you're running!" Jessica yelled. She looked at her friends and rolled her eyes. "Dennis Cookman is such a creep!"

"Really!" Janet agreed. Then she turned her attention back to Jessica's sweater. "I just love it!" she cooed.

While the Unicorns were complimenting Jessica on her sweater, Winston Egbert was running as fast as he could around the corner of the school. His long legs made him a good runner, but even so, Dennis Cookman was gaining on him. Suddenly, Winston's foot hit a rock. He tumbled forward, landing with a thud on the new-mown grass.

A second later, Dennis was on top of him, straddling Winston with his legs. "Come on, Egbert, be a pal and lend me your lunch money. I'll pay you back. I promise."

"You borrowed Ken Matthew's lunch money last week," Winston said, "but you never paid *him* back."

"Hey, don't be smart. Not unless you want me to get rough with you." He put his knee on Winston's chest and pressed down.

"Ow! Knock it off!" Winston cried.

"Hand over the money then."

"Oh, all right." Winston reached into his pocket and pulled out his lunch money. "Here."

"Thanks, pal," Dennis laughed, pocketing the money. "And don't bother telling anybody about this. Not unless you want to see more of this." He shook his fist in Winston's face and then jumped to his feet. "See you around, Egbert."

Winston crawled to his knees and watched as Dennis ran off across the lawn. His chest hurt, and he felt like crying. He wanted to tell on Dennis, but he was frightened. Dennis was mean and strong, and he wasn't afraid to prove it.

With a sigh, Winston stood up and walked back around the school. Maybe he could borrow some lunch money from one of his friends. Or maybe he'd skip lunch all together. Either way, it would be worth it to keep Dennis Cookman happy.

Will Dennis Cookman get away with bullying the entire sixth grade class? Find out in **The Bully,** *Sweet Valley Twins 19.*

We hope you enjoyed reading this book. If you would like to receive further information about titles available in the Bantam series, just write to the address below, with your name and address:

Kim Prior
Bantam Books
61–63 Uxbridge Road
Ealing
London W5 5SA

If you live in Australia or New Zealand and would like more information about the series, please write to:

Sally Porter
Transworld Publishers (Aust.) Pty. Ltd.
15–23 Helles Avenue
Moorebank
N.S.W. 2170
AUSTRALIA

Kiri Martin
Transworld Publishers (N.Z.) Ltd.
Cnr. Moselle and Waipareira Avenues
Henderson
Auckland
NEW ZEALAND

All Bantam Young Adult books are available at your bookshop or newsagent, or can be ordered from the following address:

Corgi/Bantam Books
Cash Sales Department
PO Box 11
Falmouth
Cornwall
TR10 9EN

Please list the title(s) you would like, and send together with a cheque or postal order. You should allow for the cost of the book(s) plus postage and packing charges as follows:

All orders up to a total of £5.00   50p
All orders in excess of £5.00   Free

Please note that payment must be made in pounds sterling; other currencies are unacceptable.

(The above applies to readers in the UK and Republic of Ireland only)

B.F.P.O. customers, please allow for the cost of the book(s) plus the following for postage and packing: 60p for the first book, 25p for the second book and 15p per copy for the next 7 books, thereafter 9p per book.

Overseas customers, please allow £1.25 for postage and packing for the first book, 75p for the second book, and 28p for each subsequent title ordered.

Thank you!

Janet Quin-Harkin's Sugar & Spice

Meet the most unlikely pair of best friends since Toni and Jill from Janet Quin-Harkin's TEN BOY SUMMER.

Caroline's thrilled to find out she's got a long-lost cousin exactly her age. But she's horrified when Chrissy comes to spend a year with her family. Caroline's a reserved and polite only child – now she has to share her life with a loud, unsophisticated, embarrassing farm girl!

Ask your bookseller for any titles you have missed: